loving the ladies' man

a sweet romantic comedy

kristin canary

Blue Aster
PRESS

For my husband and sons.
You are my inspiration and my joy.
Thank you for all the bookish fodder.

one

. . .

I HAVE EXACTLY THREE MONTHS, two weeks, and one day until my life potentially changes forever.

And my mother won't let me forget it.

She doesn't mean to make me feel guilty. I know that. But whenever I talk with her, I can't help but think about the approaching deadline—about the promise I made nearly a decade ago.

"I know you love California, Evie, but I just couldn't live there." We're shooting the breeze, catching up over my lunch break while I sit behind my desk eating cold leftover pizza. She's spent the last several minutes telling me about all the things that have happened this week on the Iowa dairy farm she runs with my dad—the one that's been in the Denmark family for over a century. The one I left behind to follow my own dreams. "I'd miss the rolling plains, the four seasons, the peace and quiet of home."

As I hold my phone to my ear, I take a bite of crust

and swivel in my office chair, leaning back and looking up at the familiar ceiling that's riddled with a crumbly popcorn texture and several cracks. "Actually, I kind of like the fact that it's February and I'm not freezing my rear off." I try to infuse lightness into my tone, but can't help the way it notches up, tight. "And not sure I'd exactly call it quiet there with all of those mooing cows."

"Oh, sugar." She laughs, and I can hear in her voice how much she loves me. "We sure do miss you. It's not the same without you here. Maybe you can come for a visit soon?"

"Sure, Mom. I'll try." And I feel it again, like I'm sinking, drowning in a sea of *should-I-haves*. There's nothing I hate more than hearing the disappointment in my mother's voice.

But I know it isn't just disappointment—it's need. My parents *need* me to hold up my end of the bargain. The tiny bit of money I've started sending home every month isn't enough to make much of a difference. Definitely not enough to hire another employee to give my parents a break.

Looking back, I suppose it was short-sighted to tell my parents I would move home and take over the dairy farm—the job I was groomed for since I was a kid—if I hadn't met a certain level of career success within ten years. It was even more short-sighted to define "success" as "sending home X amount of dollars every month." I cringe to think of that now, as if my self-worth can be tied to my finances.

But back then, ten years felt like a lifetime. I thought I had all the time in the world to prove to my parents—

to myself—that I could both pursue my passions *and* be the daughter they deserved.

There's a knock on my door and I sit up straight. Sally, one of my acquisitions editors, is standing in my office doorway. She waves at me and her eyes widen in that "I've got something important to discuss" look.

I hold up a finger and lower my voice. "Sorry, Mom. I've got to go."

"Of course, sweetie. Talk soon?"

"Yes. Soon." I hang up, blow out a breath, and run my hands through my waist-length brown hair that desperately needs a wash—and a trim.

But as the editorial director at Evermore Publishers, a boutique press in San Diego, I don't have time for things like haircuts. I've been working about twelve to fifteen hours every day for the last two years—ever since David broke my heart—trying to prove to my boss that I'm a valuable employee so that when a promotion finally comes along, I'm in the running.

Plus, work has been a helpful way to forget the searing loss of my ex—the one that took me by complete surprise, even though it probably shouldn't have.

I wonder if it'll help me forget the stupid wedding invitation that showed up in the mail last week …

Ugh. *Focus, Evie.*

"Hi, Sally." I wave her into the office. "What's up?"

The twenty-something ducks inside and slides into the chair on the other side of my desk. "Sorry to inter-rupt. But …" She tugs on the ends of her black bob. That's when I notice her eyes are bloodshot, her bottom lip trembling.

"Hey." I reach for a tissue and hand it to her. "What's going on?"

With a brave smile, she takes the tissue and wads it up into her fist. "It's just that …" Her voice wobbles. "I'm a bit behind on the Perry project. I'd intended to work all weekend to finish it before Monday's deadline but …" And then she starts to cry.

I jump out of my seat and round the desk, pulling my wheeled office chair with me. Then I sit and put an arm around her.

I know it's not in my job description, but I can't help but feel like my team is my family. Like Sally—along with Justine, Kelly, and Tanya—are my younger sisters. And I've got to do whatever it takes to help them succeed. To protect them. To keep them close.

And when I say it out loud, I realize I sound like a crazy person. Because these women, though younger than me, are adults and don't need their manager taking care of them. But it doesn't take a shrink to figure out that this intense need to make sure my team is okay stems from the fact that I didn't protect my own sister, once upon a time.

I squeeze Sally's shoulders again. "But what?"

"Well, the story is so beautiful and I've loved working on it, but John just …" Her breath is coming in spurts now. "He just broke up with me yesterday, and I can't—absolutely can't—bring myself to keep working on a story that's got a happy ending. Not right now."

"I can understand how that would be really difficult." John … Wait, John? I thought her boyfriend was named Steve or something like that. "How long were you together?"

"T-two whole weeks!" Sally blows her red nose into the tissue. Mascara is now running down her cheeks and she looks like some sort of creepy clown.

I let her cry for a few more minutes while I rub her back. Because I understand this, the heartache of losing someone you love. Sure, some would say that two weeks is nothing compared to the years I invested in my relationship with David. But if you think someone is the one, and it turns out he isn't, it doesn't matter how long you were together. It hurts.

So it stands to reason that Sally might be hurting just as much as I did. Who am I to judge? "What can I do to help?" I mentally scan our editorial schedule. "We could maybe extend the deadline by a few days."

Sally shakes her head vehemently. "I don't think that will help. I … I can't work on any romances right now."

"But …" Evermore solely publishes romantic fiction. There are literally no other projects I *can* give her. "What do you suggest?"

She peeks up at me. "Could I take some time off next week? It would be really helpful for me to visit my family in Los Angeles. You understand, don't you? Family is so important."

Sure, drive the knife in deeper, Sally. Of course, she doesn't know all the ways I'm currently failing my own family. "Yes, that's absolutely fine. You have some vacation days, right?"

There she goes biting her lip again. "Maybe one or two."

I hold back a sigh. "That's fine. I'll approve the extra time."

"Oh, thank you so much." She throws her arms around my neck for a quick hug. But then she pulls back, brow furrowed. "What about the Perry project?"

"Don't worry about it. Just email me your notes so far." I guess I'll be spending my evening buried in the historical love story of Lady Elizabeth Williams and Lord Isaac Fairfax. There are worse ways to spend my time—she's right that it's a beautiful book, and from one of our more seasoned authors—but I was really looking forward to a movie night at home with my four housemates. It's taken us weeks to find a night that will work with all of our schedules and now I get to be the one to disappoint my friends.

My stomach tightens just thinking about it.

Sally stands and wipes away the residual mascara on her face. She suddenly seems much more chipper, lighter, even. "Oh, by the way, Lisa said she needed to see you."

"All right." What could my boss want? Normally, she just sends me an IM or email if she wants an update on a project. "Thanks."

"No problem." Sally turns and fairly skips from the room. Just the thought of seeing her family must be enough to make her feel better.

I lock my computer and head out of my tiny office into the hallway with blue carpet that has to have been around longer than I've been alive (and do I want to know what kind of dirt and germs are embedded in the carpet that's more than thirty-two years old? No, I do not). I arrive at Lisa's door, knock, and pop my head inside her office.

Lisa Chambers—Evermore's publisher (aka, head honcho)—is standing beside the large picture window that gives a picturesque view of downtown San Diego several miles away. Our office may be ancient and located in an out-of-the-way, decrepit business complex abutting a mountain, but it offers the most fantastic views you can imagine.

"Hi." I attempt to straighten my rumpled cotton skirt, which is a bit crooked from my quick walk over. "Sorry, I just heard you needed to see me."

Lisa waves her hand. "Not a problem. Come on in." Today her silver-threaded hair is pulled back into a bun, which makes her high cheekbones even more pronounced than usual. She's a five-foot-three power-house in a silky emerald-green blouse, a black jacket with three-quarter sleeves, and sleek black pants that probably cost more than I make in a month.

As I sit in one of the leather chairs across from her broad oak desk, I double check my white blouse to ensure Sally's mascara didn't stain it. Whew. All clear.

I cross and then uncross my legs. "So, all of our projects are on track to meet deadlines. As you know, we've just acquired two new titles and I'm very excited about one in particular." Lisa stays quiet, just keeps staring out the window, so that must not be what she wants to discuss. Is she leaving it up to me to figure it out? She does that sometimes, and I hate it. I clear my throat. "Is this a good time to ask about the budget meeting yesterday? Because I was a bit confused by the—"

"Evie." Lisa turns from the window, wearing an amused look. "Breathe."

"Right." I close my eyes for a minute, inhaling, imagining myself doing yoga. But who am I kidding? Yoga is totally Kayla and Lauren's thing. The one time they dragged me along to yoga on the beach, I ended up with a bloody nose after a downward-facing dog pose went awry.

"Sorry I'm late."

My eyes pop open at the deep male voice that suddenly reverberates through the room. I smell Connor before I see him, his citrusy cologne with hints of cedarwood and bergamot making my toes curl of their own accord inside my low-heeled pumps.

Marketing director Connor Bryant breezes through the door and sits in the chair next to me. I peek at him from the corner of my eye. A man should not be allowed to be as sexy as he is, with that brown hair styled to perfection and that five o'clock scruff dusting his tan, chiseled jaw. His black designer-cut suit fits him like a glove, serving to outline the broad shoulders of a guy who has clearly been an athlete all his life.

If I were ever to see him with his shirt off—*don't even picture it, Evie!*—he would definitely have a six-pack lurking under the crisp dark blue shirt that brings out the piercing quality of his gold-flecked brown eyes.

Too bad his sexiness is only skin deep.

Oh, plenty of women in our office, from Kim in accounting to Chelsea in sales to Bridgette in legal, rave about Connor's personality too. ("*He's the whole package, you guys!*") I don't know if the rumors are true that he's gone to drinks (and done who knows what else) with several of the women in the office, but he obviously enjoys his position as the only male at Evermore excepting seventy-year-old Jorge in subsidiary rights.

So yeah, Connor may have a pretty face, but when I look at him, I just see a ginormous flirt who leads women on—and I despise a man like that.

Especially when he keeps a woman on the hook for years. When he makes her think he's just as into her as she is him. When the whole time he's dating her, he is actually falling for her friend.

Oh, wait. I was talking about Connor, wasn't I?

Not David.

Still. Men like him can't be trusted.

Connor lifts his stupidly sexy eyes in acknowledgment of me for a split second before turning a crooked grin toward Lisa. "To what do we owe the pleasure of your summons, oh Fearless Leader?"

Here we go.

But instead of rolling my eyes at his sweet talk like I really want to do, I act the professional and flit on a smile to match his, straightening in my seat as if that will make me more than the frumpy workaholic he must see me as. "Yes, Lisa, can't wait to hear what all of this is about!"

Connor snorts at my peppy timbre, but I ignore him and keep focused on Lisa, who finally sits and places her folded hands on the desktop. My heart skitters in that moment. It's not abnormal for her to meet with

Connor and me at the same time, but this meeting was unscheduled.

Unplanned.

And I absolutely hate it when things are sprung on me. My mind flashes to the invitation tucked under a stack of papers on my desk back in my office. *Stephanie Lamb and David Atkinson invite you to join their wedding celebration …*

I shudder and refocus on Lisa, whose lips are moving. Oh no. I missed whatever it is she said.

"… and that's why I've narrowed down my pool of contenders to the two of you."

Huh? Contenders for what?

My eyes dart between Lisa and Connor, who strokes his long fingers down the sides of his face and chin. "Thank you for having such faith in us, Lisa. We won't let you down."

When both of their gazes float in my direction, I nod, a tad too enthusiastic (especially for someone who has no idea what was said). But there's no way I can admit I wasn't listening. "Absolutely."

"Wonderful. So I'll be watching you both even more closely." Lisa turns to face her computer, then flicks her eyes back to us. "Go on, then. Back to work, my dream team."

Connor stands and I follow suit, all the way into the hallway. Before he can return to his office, I place my hand on his upper arm. And *ho boy*. His bicep underneath my fingers is rock hard. I know he works as much as I do, so how in the world does this guy find time to get arms like *this*? Maybe he does pushups in his office in between conference calls.

My armpits are suddenly sweating at the mental image.

"Yeah?" His six-two frame doesn't exactly tower over me—after all, I'm five-nine. But I feel as small as a mouse facing a mountain when I look up into those same eyes that are every woman's fantasy.

Every *other* woman, that is.

I quickly remove my hand. "So I was a bit distracted in there." Flexing the fingers that just touched Connor, I rub them with my other hand. "I didn't hear what Lisa said."

"Which part?" Arms crossed over his chest, he leans against the hallway wall, regarding me with an air of coolness—his *modus operandi* when it comes to our interactions in private.

"Um … all of it?"

He laughs, incredulous.

Why did I ever think to ask him for help? "Forget it. I'll just …" Sure that my face resembles a tomato, I turn on my heel to retreat to my office.

"Wait."

I stop, pivot back to face him, eyebrows raised.

He runs a hand through his hair. Lucky hand. (*Stop it, Evie! So he's attractive! Get over it.*) "She said that she's opening up an associate publisher position around Memorial Day—when the budget will allow for it—and she wants to promote from within."

Associate publisher would be a significant step up for me. More responsibilities, little to no editing, but it would come with better benefits, including a larger paycheck.

Exactly what I need to finally fulfill the promise I made to my parents.

And just in time too, because Memorial Day is about three months away.

I tap my foot against the ground. "And she's going to promote one of us?"

"That's right." A tiny smile curls the edges of his lips.

What? Does he think he's got the job in the bag? I mean, yeah, if Lisa is selecting someone based on how well they can schmooze, Connor will for sure be her top pick.

But I work just as hard, if not harder, than he does. My team seems to like me all right. I know the business inside and out. And I'm a darn good editor.

Yes. I'd be a good choice too.

That's right, Evie. Keep telling yourself you have a chance against Mr. Charming.

I swallow hard. "So one of us will become the other's boss?" Just what I need—and I don't know which scenario would be worse. Somehow having to manage Connor or having a boss I don't respect.

"She was a bit murky on those details. Said most likely she'd keep at least one of our positions as a direct report for herself. She just needs someone to share the load."

Whew. Tugging at the bottom of my shirt, I nod. "Thanks for filling me in."

"Of course." He studies me for a moment, then extends his hand. "May the best person win."

"Right." When I touch his skin with my own, something in my legs becomes soft, like melting ice. And yet Connor doesn't seem affected at all. He pulls his hand away and turns back toward his office.

Just as I'm retreating into my own, I hear him greet our receptionist, June. He's over-the-top friendly and I turn my head at the last minute to see him leaning over her desk, plucking a piece of chocolate from her dish and laughing when she punches him playfully in the shoulder.

In the ten years that we've worked together, he's never once acted like that with me. In fact, other than Lisa, I might just be the only woman in the office he's never flirted with.

But you know what? That's fine. I mean, at one point, I might have welcomed his attention (back when I was naive). But then I had David, and that relationship consumed me for three years.

And if David taught me anything, it's that I can't trust my own judgment when it comes to smooth-talking men.

Now, I'm focusing on my career—either I'll get this job and stay here in California, or Connor will get promoted and I'll get a one-way ticket back to Iowa, having failed in my mission to send my parents enough money for the farm.

Sure, my dream job will be in the rearview mirror, but at least they won't have to suffer anymore for their daughter's selfish choices.

I've already cost them their oldest daughter. I can't cost them their livelihood—their home—as well.

Blinking against hot liquid threatening to fall down my cheeks, I peel my eyes off of the scene unfolding in the front lobby and step firmly into my office, closing the door and plopping into my chair.

As I wake up the computer screen, download Sally's notes, and put my eyes on the historical manuscript she sent over, I slowly lose myself in the story. My breath comes easier and my pulse slows.

And yet, in the back of my mind, there pounds a steady thought.

Somehow, I have to beat Connor—but I don't know if I can.

two

COFFEE IS MY LIFEBLOOD.

I really wish I liked tea instead. Tea feels so much more sophisticated, so much more ... I don't know. Literary.

As someone whose favorite book is and will forever remain *Pride & Prejudice*, I could so imagine myself sitting in a gorgeous Regency-style drawing room with Elizabeth Bennet sipping from our delicate china cups and discussing our favorite poetry.

Sigh. Everything about the Regency era sounds better. Well, except for the corsets and voluminous dresses. Give me my knit skirts and sweaters any day, thank you very much. (And who cares if others think I look like the world's non-sexiest librarian? I happen to like being comfortable.)

Alas, not only does tea have too little caffeine to keep my engines running (remember, I work an insane amount!), but it simply lacks the same bold flavor of an americano. Plus my dad started slinging coffee at me when I was fourteen and was having trouble getting out of bed at the ungodly hour of four a.m. to milk the cows, so I'm basically pre-conditioned to like the stuff.

Which is why I'm completely at home inside Java Awakening, the little coffee shop and bakery five miles from my office. It's where I come to escape from the stresses of my job—and where I meet up several times a week with my roommate and best friend, Kayla Clark.

A few hours after my meeting with Lisa and Connor, I pull open the coffee shop door and am met with a blast of air laden with the smell of dark roast beans and chocolate. Immediately, my shoulders relax as I breathe in the familiar sweetness. Overhead, there's music playing, some sort of soothing pop song that I'm not hip enough to know the name of.

Patrons are spread out at industrial-looking black tables, talking in groups or reading or working at their laptops with headphones in. My heels click on the wooden floors as I make my way to the counter, where an array of my favorite sweets are displayed. Maybe I'll treat myself to a chocolate croissant today. My waistline may not need it, but my spirits do.

I wait behind a woman with red hair harrumphing into her phone and study the handwritten chalkboard menu hanging behind the register. Just as the redhead is stepping up to order, someone tugs on my elbow and I turn to find Kayla.

I give her a quick hug. "You're early." I usually arrive about ten minutes before she does and order our drinks.

"I had to get away from the Wicked Witch." Kayla is as sleek and gorgeous as ever, her highlighted light brown hair perfectly styled in waves around her shoulders, her green eyes made brighter by the vibrant red dress she's wearing. Somehow it's both stylish and professional, with some sort of high-waisted belt and light, fluttery material that skims her legs—legs that are made even longer by the four-inch heels she's wearing.

I instantly feel sorry for her, and not just because of how much her feet must be hurting. "What's she done now?"

We've all had a less-than-desirable boss at some point in our lives, right? I had one in college who constantly mixed up my schedule and made me work every weekend night shift, letting the prettier girls off the hook whenever they asked because they had "exciting plans" and boring Evie Denmark was just going to study anyway.

But Kayla's boss Miranda might literally be the spawn of Satan. Not only is she a sexist—ironically only giving promotions to the handsome male attorneys at the law firm she owns—but she once made Kayla finish up a brief while recovering from an emergency appendectomy in the hospital.

The woman is always pulling stuff like that at all hours of the day and night. Kayla is basically "on" twenty-four-seven. But because it's a good-paying job that's allowing her to pay off her massive law school debt, she stays.

Even though Lisa expects us to work hard, she's always been fair and considerate. And suddenly, I'm even more grateful for the fact that I got in on the ground level at Evermore just out of college, only a year after it opened its doors. It's how I was able to move up from editorial assistant to full-blown editorial director in such a short time.

"What's she done? Nothing out of the norm. Just being Miranda." The tightness in Kayla's face eases as she shakes out her hands and turns to face the counter. The red-haired woman moves to the side and it's our turn.

Together, we step forward and Josh—the barista who is always working when we come in—greets us with a quiet smile. "Afternoon, ladies. You want the usual?"

His gaze lingers on Kayla, who doesn't seem to notice. Behind his thick-rimmed glasses, I sense a sort of puppy dog-esque longing on his face. And sure, with his skinny jeans and the hipster vibe he's got going on, he's not exactly Kayla's type, but from what I've seen of him over the last few years since we discovered Java Awakening, he's a really sweet guy.

Since Kayla isn't saying anything, I smile at him—trying to communicate with my lips and eyes what I can't say out loud. *Sorry about my friend. She's oblivious.* "Yep, americano for me, please. Gotta fuel up for a late evening."

That gets Kayla's attention. "You need coffee to stay awake for a girls' night?" She smirks. "Are we that boring?"

At my cringe, she frowns, pointing her finger at me. "No, Evie. You can't work."

"I have to."

"Says who?"

"One of my editors has a … family emergency." Well, kind of. "I have to take over a project for her, and the only way I can fit it in is to work on it this weekend."

Kayla groans.

Josh clears his throat. Oh yeah. We're in the middle of ordering. How rude are we? "Sorry, Josh. Um, can you please throw in a croissant?"

"No worries. Sorry to hear you'll be working late." Josh hits a few buttons on the register. "Anything else?"

"Kay?" I elbow my friend. "What do you want? It's my turn to pay."

"No, it's mine." She looks at Josh, a firm set to her chin. "It's mine."

He chuckles and holds up his hands. "I'm staying out of this one."

I roll my eyes. "You paid last time."

Kayla pulls out her wallet. Ignoring me, she speaks directly to Josh again. "I'll take a mocha, please. Here." She shoves her credit card into his hand and turns back to me. "You have to save every penny if you're going to be able to afford the bungalow."

I freeze. "What bungalow?"

"The one a few streets over that you've been eyeing for years. It's on the market, and from what I can tell from looking at it online, it needs a lot of repairs. Maybe you could get it for a decent price."

Anything in California is not what I'd consider "a decent price," since I grew up in Iowa, but I eagerly dig out my phone and step away from the counter. As I look up the one-bedroom bungalow on my web browser, I make my way to our usual table in the corner.

When Kayla arrives a few minutes later with our drinks and my croissant, I've already perused all of the pictures and my heart is pounding. She's totally right. Even though I make beans, with the right loan, this might be within my price range. I can just picture myself in the adorable dwelling. Well, once I apply new paint and patch up the holes in the walls and maybe put down new laminate …

But then my chest deflates. What am I thinking? "I can't afford this." I take a sip of my coffee and enjoy the bold flavor zapping my tongue. "You know all of my extra money goes to my parents right now. Even if I got the promotion, I'm not sure if I'd be able to afford the house *and* an extra employee at the farm."

"Promotion?" Kayla's eyebrows make a V as she sits back in her chair and drums manicured nails across the tabletop.

"Yeah, to associate publisher. I just found out today that I'm being considered." As we drink our coffee, I tell her about my meeting. "But you know Connor will probably get the job."

"And why do I know that?" Kayla picks a small flaky bit off the edge of the croissant sitting between us and pops it into her mouth.

"Because, he's Connor. He wins everyone over with his charm."

"Everyone except you, apparently."

"Right." I tear off a chunk of the pastry and take a bite then a quick sip of coffee, unable to hold back a groan of pleasure. Okay, forget living in Jane Austen's time. Give me americanos and croissants or give me death.

"Evie." Kayla waits for me to look at her before proceeding. "You need to have more confidence in yourself. You're an amazing editor and leader. And you could be even more amazing if you didn't let everyone walk all over you."

"I don't do that!" Oops, a bit of coffee sputters out with my exclamation, but seriously. I snag a napkin from the table's dispenser and wipe up the evidence that I'm as messy as a toddler. "I just try to help out whenever I can."

"Those women make up crazy excuses to get you to do their work for them, and you let it happen!" Shaking her head, she pats my arm as if I'm one of her clients whose husbands cheated on them for years before they caught on.

I mean, sure, my team does seem to need help an awful lot, and sometimes their excuses are eye-roll-worthy. But honestly? I love working with words. Being an editor—helping to shape stories, to make them better—has always been my dream and I think I'd be happy to die with a red pen in my hand (because yes, I am totally that old soul who often will print out manuscripts and correct them by hand). So I don't really mind when my team asks me to pitch in on a project, even if it adds a bit of stress when juggling multiple deadlines at once.

"Do you even want to be an associate publisher? Wouldn't you have to worry about sales and be more about overall branding instead of actually working with the manuscripts?"

It's like the woman has spy bots in my brain, although I suppose sharing space for the last seven years in our three-bedroom house in Point Loma—where five of us live, and Kayla is my roomie—is probably why she can read me so well.

And I could try to pretend I don't know what she's talking about, but she would know I'm lying and call me on it, so there's no point. I sigh. "I'm not sure, to be honest. I do think there are a lot of parts I'd like, though I would miss the day-in-and-day-out editing. But I can't keep working the same job. It's just not an option."

"Why not? You're happy, aren't you?"

"I mean, I love what I do. You know that." I bite my lip. "But if I don't make more money, I have to leave California."

"Oh, come on." Kayla rolls her eyes. She's such a compassionate friend, I tell you. "Your parents will love you even if you don't move home."

"I know that." I do. Really. My mom and dad are the best people I know. They love each other fiercely, something I strive to have in a marriage someday. And they love me just as much.

They loved—love—Janelle too.

And I'm the reason she's gone.

I shake off the gloom that always appears alongside thoughts of my sister. "But I made a promise, and I don't break my promises."

"Look, Evie." Kayla leans forward, poised to pounce, and puts on her scary listen-to-me-I'm-a-lawyer voice.

"I'm guessing your parents don't even remember you making that stupid promise, and I'll never understand your reason for making it in the first place. I guess you felt the need to make yourself feel better about coming out here, but why should you feel guilty about leaving the nest and pursuing your dream? Isn't that every parent's dream for their kid?"

"You know why I made the promise." My voice is low, trembling.

She sighs and, in a move that's very uncharacteristic of Kayla, she takes my hand across the table. Squeezes it. "I know why you *think* you had to make the promise, but your sister's death isn't your fault."

I open my mouth to protest, but shut it again with one lawyerly look from my best friend.

"Your parents want you to be happy—and you *are.* Here."

Pushing away a hot tear that falls down my cheek, I shake my head. "And *because* they want me to be happy, they'll never tell me the truth, but I know it all the same. They're both getting older and can't handle all the work like they used to, so they need my money or they need me. They need help, Kay."

My americano has gone lukewarm by this point, but I down it anyway because I'll be lucky to get home before midnight. If only they sold IVs filled with the stuff. Then I could hook myself up at my desk and be set for life.

I stand, decision made. "I can't let them down, which means I have to get the job. And that means that the bungalow is off the table."

"You're a much better daughter than I am." Kayla grunts. "I hope your parents appreciate you."

I smile, but it's weak. The fact is, I don't really care about being appreciated.

I only care about being absolved.

three

· · ·

MY AMERICANO WORE off hours ago. The time has come—I must resort to break-room coffee.

I click Save on my computer and stand to stretch. My back twinges and my stomach gurgles, not surprising since it's been something like eight hours since I ate at one o'clock. Maybe it's time to order some food for delivery and take a break. I've hit a wall in this story anyway. Turns out Sally wasn't as far along as I thought she'd be, and I'm basically starting from scratch.

I snag my favorite coffee mug, which has a picture of Colin Firth, aka the real Mr. Darcy, saying:

Hey girl, don't mind me.

I'm just admiring your fine eyes even though I hate your family.

And by the way, will you marry me?

Makes me smile every time.

Since I kicked off my shoes hours ago, I step into the hallway barefoot. At this time of day (or should I say night), the fluorescent lighting has dimmed and there's a quiet hum coming from somewhere. Other than that, there's no sound. I'm alone and it's peaceful. Just the way I like to work.

I find my way into the break room that consists of a fridge, a small counter with a sink and a commercial coffee maker, a few tables and chairs, and a vending machine. Methodically, I add the filter and ingredients to the coffee machine and wait for the brown sludge to drip into the pot. While the liquid plinks into the glass, I walk to the window at the edge of the break room and stare up at the mountain that backs our building. Thanks to the full moon, I can make out an abundance of rocks and tall trees. Several houses stand sentinel on the mountainside, the scattered lights a reminder that other people are spending their Friday evening at home.

I think back to the texted picture I received about an hour ago from Kayla—her, squished together on a couch with fitness instructor Lauren, kindergarten teacher Shelby, and purple-haired graphic artist Alexis—all making kissy faces at me.

Sighing, I find my way back to the coffee pot, grab my mug, pour myself a cuppa, and stare into Mr. Darcy's gorgeous brown eyes. "Looks like it's just you and me tonight, Fitzwilliam."

And then, Mr. Darcy betrays me.

Or rather, the ground beneath me does.

There's a sudden large jolt and my coffee sloshes over the side of the mug, dousing my white shirt with hot liquid. A curse that would make my mama blush—and yes, Mr. Darcy too—flies out of my mouth. But before I can even think about peeling off the blouse to check for third-degree burns, the floor shakes.

Hard.

Fast.

I drop the mug and it breaks at my feet.

The table and chair legs make such a racket as they bounce that I toss my hands over my ears before I fall to the ground, unable to keep my feet underneath me. Plates and cups fall from the cupboards over the sink, adding to the noise.

I squeeze my eyes shut. This is how I die—alone, at work, with Mr. Darcy in shattered pieces around me.

I'm sure there's a metaphor in there somewhere.

But before I know it, the shaking stops. The lights overhead flicker, then go dark. It takes a few seconds, but half the lights come back on.

I stand, shaky, using the counter to support me. Other than some knocked-over chairs and the broken dishes, nothing else seems to have been affected by what is the first real earthquake I've experienced in my time here in California. My head swims and I blink rapidly, trying to clear away the tears I don't remember crying.

Still, I'm safe. I'm whole—albeit a mess.

For a minute, I just breathe. But then I hear some sort of distant rumbling. Is that normal after an earthquake? An aftershock, maybe? Do they come this quickly on the heels of the initial shaking? I should have done more research on what to do in this situation. Oh, well. Too late now.

Taking a step, I wince at a sudden pain in my foot.

Oh look, my big toe is bleeding from the broken mug. But I don't have time to think about that. I limp toward the window—and what I see makes my blood run cold.

Trees snap and boulders fall, rolling as the land slides and rushes—right toward the building where I'm standing.

I turn and run back toward the door, dodging a table as I go and crying out when I step once again on the broken bits of Mr. Darcy. But nothing prepares me for the sound of glass breaking behind me.

A scream comes from somewhere and it takes me a minute to figure out that it's me—I'm the one making the high-pitched noise. But as I glance back, it's with good reason, because a large jagged tree branch is now poking half inside the fifth-story window where I was just seconds ago.

More glass breaks in other parts of the building and I start to hyperventilate. The air in my lungs feels tight and I gulp for it. Gulp again. Where can I go? What if the dirt and mud come surging inside? Is that how it works? Can the whole mountain come down on top of me?

Maybe I really will die here all alone. And what will my friends and family put on my tombstone?

Here lies Evie Denmark.

She worked a lot and still had nothing to show for it.

All of her efforts weren't any good to anyone.

"Oh, God. Help. Help."

One second, I'm crouched in a ball in the middle of the kitchen, shivering and alone. The next, strong arms are around me and I'm suddenly warm. So warm.

And I don't even care that I've died, because heaven smells really, really good. Almost like …

My head pops up. "Connor?"

Sure enough, he's squatting beside me, his dark brow furrowed. Other than the fact his tie is loosened in that sexy *honey-I'm-home* look, he is the same—unflustered and completely put together—as he was earlier today. Completely the opposite of how I'm sure I appear.

And it's then I realize that the rumbling has stopped. Well, the rumbling outside the building.

The rumbling inside my body is stronger than ever.

I slump fully onto my bottom and the cold tile seeps through my skirt onto the backs of my legs. "What are you doing here?"

He looks at my feet and frowns. "You're bleeding." His gaze roams my whole body from there, stopping at my torso before he quickly averts his eyes.

I glance down and gasp. Thanks to my run-in with spilled coffee, my white shirt is plastered to my chest—and completely see-through. Fabulous! My lacy pink bra (the one sexy thing I own) is basically on display for the whole world to see.

Or just Connor. But still!

My cheeks heating, I turn a complete one-eighty on my butt so my back is to him. "You didn't answer my question." And yes, my voice is a bit growly, but how should a girl who's just been through a terrifying earthquake talk? "What are you doing here?"

"The same as you, I'd guess. Working late."

And then something like silk surrounds my whole

body and the scent of Connor's cologne is stronger than ever. He's given me his suit jacket. I mumble a thank you as I slip my arms inside and fumble to fasten the large buttons. I'm not a petite girl but I'm still swimming in it. Thankfully though, it covers up my traitorous shirt.

The wind is howling from the broken window on the other side of the kitchen. I turn back to face Connor, but he's already standing at the kitchen counter, rummaging through the cabinets and grabbing something off the top shelf before moving toward me again. He sinks down, a first-aid kit in hand. The adrenaline is slowly dissipating from my veins, but that doesn't stop the electric currents that flow from his fingers to my right foot as he gently lifts it closer to his face to examine my cuts.

"What are you doing?"

His lips quirk in that oh-so-Connor way. "Just making sure you don't have any glass stuck in there."

"Shouldn't we call 911 or something?"

"I already tried when I saw the landslide start. Couldn't get through. I'm sure the phone lines are jam-packed with calls. Not just to emergency personnel, but to family and friends too. They tend to get overwhelmed right after an emergency like this."

"Oh." I wouldn't have thought of that.

"Don't worry. We're safe for now."

Safe, huh? I shove his hand away. "I'll feel a lot safer when I'm out of this building and back home."

"Can you even walk?"

"I'm fine. Let's just go downstairs and get out of here

before the earth decides to tilt again." I try to stand, but cry out at the pain in my feet.

"Whoa, there." Somehow, Connor leaps to his feet and catches me before I fall.

My hands grip the front of his blue button-up work shirt—and hello, rock-hard chest. Nice to meet you. I'm not sure how long I stand there stupidly leaning on the parts of my feet that aren't stinging, my fingers splayed across his pectoral muscles. All I know is I'm completely mortified when Connor clears his throat and breaks the spell that his hotness has cast over me.

I squeak out a *sorry* before sitting on the ground again.

"Unfortunately, I don't think we're going anywhere for a while." He takes it in stride and lowers himself beside me once more. "Before I knew you were in here, I was watching out the window from my office and saw the landslide block the front doors and the emergency exit." He opens an antiseptic wipe and unfolds the square. "Do you want to do this or should I?"

"I can." Because letting him touch me again is a really bad idea right now. I've read waaaay too many romance novels and my imagination is going a teensy bit wild. *Remember, you don't even like this guy. It doesn't matter that he rescued you and is hotter than hades on a summer day or that he gave you his jacket like some sort of freaking Prince Charming.* "Thanks."

Thankfully, the cuts aren't super deep, just painful. I take the wipe from him and dab at the two largest gashes, one on my left big toe and another on the arch of my right foot. Hissing at the contact, I bite my lip. And there goes my dumb hand trembling again. What in the world is wrong with me?

Oh, I don't know. You almost died, that's what.

Stop being so dramatic, Evie.

You *stop being so dramatic.*

Oh, dear. I've turned into a raving lunatic, talking to myself in my own mind.

Fortunately, Connor has no idea of my inner turmoil. Or maybe he does, because without a word, he eases the wipe from my fingers and finishes cleaning the wounds. Then he gently applies antibiotic cream and bandages. "There. All better."

I swallow, my throat parched. "Thank you." Blowing out a breath, I play with a button on Connor's jacket, which I'm still wearing. "So, we're stuck?"

"For now. We could try seeing if there's a window we can climb out of, but since the upper windows don't open, we'd have to go through a broken one." Connor stands again and throws away the trash, putting the first-aid kit back in the cabinet. "I'll try calling 911 again in a bit, but I'm guessing we might be spending the night here at least."

Evie, don't think about the book you just edited. You know, the one where the hero and heroine get stuck overnight in a village apothecary shop and—

Oh my.

I said DON'T think about it!

Right. Gah. Shaking myself from the reverie, I fan my face with the excess material from Connor's sleeve. "Okay. Well, it seems we still have some power." Maybe no internet, but thankfully I don't need that to do some basic editing. "I guess I'll just get back to my work."

Connor nods. "Sounds good. I'll let you know when I get through to 911." He helps me to my feet, but when I grimace, he scoops me up and I'm literally floating until he deposits me into my office chair.

Then before I can even thank him, he's gone.

And the silence I once found peaceful now deafens me.

four

THIS IS POINTLESS.

It's only been a few hours since Connor dropped me off, and in between texting my friends and family—my phone won't make calls, but can send messages for some reason—all I've done is sit at my desk, staring at my computer. No matter how hard I try to focus on Elizabeth and Isaac, the only story I care about at the moment is the one that has me trapped inside a building practically starving.

Because it's been hours since I ate. And did I mention I'm starving?

Also, my feet hurt despite the two Advil I downed when I got back to my office.

Also also, I'm still shaken from my near-death experience. And yes, I'm aware that I'm being dramatic—and it's embarrassing, okay?

I've tried to avoid the internet, which is working

after all, because my nerves are still a bit too raw to flip through stories about the damage caused by the earthquake. But according to Kayla, it wasn't actually as high on the Richter scale as it felt. There are definitely areas of town that got it worse than others, like where Connor and I are, and ours isn't the only landslide. It's too early to tell if a lot of people are injured or just as lucky as Connor and me.

So for now, I wait.

My stomach grumbles for the eightieth time (see? soooo dramatic!) and I finally swivel away from my computer. "All right, all right. You win." I ease out of Connor's jacket and check my shirt. Stained, but dry.

Then, as slowly as possible, I try to put weight on my feet.

Nope, nope, nope.

I sit. Gritting my teeth, I turn my feet so I'm walking on the outside of each like a strange kind of monkey. I make it to the door—oh so proud of myself—before the bones in my feet start to really hurt.

That's it. I have no choice.

I drop to my knees and crawl toward the break room. Although I have no food in the fridge, maybe one of my co-workers will have left something behind. Of course, under normal circumstances I would never dream of stealing someone else's food, but this is most definitely not normal. Especially because Connor could pop out of his office at any moment and see me. That will surely add to his stellar opinion of me.

Although honestly, I'm guessing he doesn't think

about me at all. He's probably sad he's not stuck instead with one of the many rail-thin beauties who work here. A past—or present—fling.

As I crawl, I try to ignore the fact that I'm now super close to the nasty carpet I was just thinking about earlier today and that it smells like a combo between wet dog and the flowers that bloom on the orange tree outside of my window every spring. My hair swings forward, touching the ground. Ew, ew, ew. I try to move forward, but keep tripping over it.

Well, this won't work.

I stop to tie my hair in a knot on top of my head— and thank goodness it's so caked with dry shampoo today, because it actually stays. I mean, I'm sure I look like some sort of bride of Frankenstein, but desperate times, right?

Sweat starts to form at my temple as I continue my trek down the hallway. Seriously, when did it get so long? My knees are aching and little bits of debris are digging into my flesh.

A door opens somewhere behind me. "Please no, no, no," I whisper.

"Going somewhere?"

Aw, come on. Couldn't I have maintained just a tiny bit of dignity in all of this? Maybe if I ignore Connor, he'll go away. I put my head back down and keep crawling like I'm in the army and this is basic training.

But in a flash, he's standing directly in front of me. "Why are you crawling?" If I'm not mistaken, there's amusement in Connor's tone.

Oh, sure. Laugh at the injured girl. Maybe sometime in the distant future, I'll be able to laugh at this too. But right now? I'm so not in the mood. Part of it is the hunger that's inducing a headache and twisting my stomach into knots. Add to that the lingering anxiety over our entire situation here and it's a fierce mixture—which is why I can't help the biting tone in my voice. "Move, Connor."

"Whoa there, Evie. No need to get testy." I've heard that teasing tone before, when he flirts with women. But he's not flirting right now. He's mocking me.

Isn't he?

The confusion makes my head hurt even more. "I said, move."

I need food. Stat.

"Where are you going?" He pauses, but just for a second. "Do you need me to carry you?"

For the love of all that is good, just let me pass. "To the break room for food. And no, I'm perfectly capable of doing it on my own."

"I can see that." He's still standing in front of me as he chuckles.

That's it. I'm out of options, and I tried being reasonable …

I head butt his legs.

He lets loose a disbelieving laugh as he falls onto his butt and bangs his elbow against the wall.

I sit up on my knees, eyes wide. In my haze of hunger, I've gone too far. "Oh no. I'm so sorry. Are you okay?"

"What did you do that for?" He's rubbing his arm

and staring at me like I'm the most confounding creature he's ever seen.

I press the palms of my hands against my closed eyes for a moment. "I was hangry." Then I peek at him again.

Sitting this close to him, I can see the gold rimming his eyes.

Still rubbing his elbow, he cocks his head. "Hangry?"

"Yes. You know. Hungry and angry?" I bite my lip. Surely he understands.

But he just shakes his head. "I wouldn't think an editor would use made-up words."

"She would if no real word existed to adequately describe the state in which she finds herself—and right now, that state is hangry. You were blocking me from my quarry, so I tried to move you."

I shrug and attempt to look apologetic. Because I am. Sort of. On another level, it was kind of nice to finally knock Connor Bryant down a peg—literally. "But I didn't mean to hurt you."

After a few long seconds of blinking at me, his face breaks out into a huge grin. "Quarry. Now that's more like it, Webster."

My nose wrinkles. "Webster?"

"Like the dictionary?" Connor stands, dusts off his pants, and holds out a hand to me. "Come on. I'll help you get to the kitchen and we can get some food into you. Then I can update you on my call with emergency services."

Now he has my attention. I stand and allow him to pick me up again, trying to ignore how good it feels to be momentarily nestled against a man's chest. It's been so long …

He's just being polite, Evie.

I clear my thoughts and refocus on what Connor said about emergency services. "So you got through?"

He walks the rest of the way down the hallway to the break room and sets me down in a chair. "Yeah, finally." Heading to the fridge, he rummages around. "I was just coming to get you when I saw your … journey to the break room."

I'm never going to live that down. I just pray he doesn't tell the rest of the office. He'll probably describe it to everyone at our next staff meeting. "What did they say?"

Connor emerges from the fridge with two plastic containers, removes the lids, and sticks the Tupperware into the microwave. "Not surprisingly, they have a long list of emergencies and well checks to perform before getting to us." While the food is heating, Connor faces me again and leans back against the counter.

"Why are we so far down on the list?"

"We aren't, necessarily. The list is just long. They have a lot of people in more dire situations than us, and when I told them we were mostly okay, they said they'd have someone out as quickly as possible. But it may not be until tomorrow. Possibly Sunday."

I'm seriously going to stink if I don't get a shower for forty-eight hours. I probably already do, unlike Connor, the poster boy for a cologne ad.

But that's a super shallow thing to think about right now. After all, we're safe, have a plethora of vending machine food, and cell phone service. Everything else is just a minor inconvenience.

"Aren't they concerned about land shifting even more during the aftershocks?" I try not to think too hard about the possibility that more damage could occur—that we aren't really safe after all.

The microwave whirs behind him. "I guess it could happen, but apparently that's a risk they're willing to take."

"I'm assuming that there's no way out of here on our own?"

"Not that I could find. Access to the outside via the stairwell door is totally blocked by rocks, and there aren't any open windows on what is now the ground floor."

"Boo."

"Yeah." The microwave beeps, so Connor removes the heated containers and brings them to the table where I'm sitting. He places one in front of me. It's a creamy chicken pasta dish that smells divine—like something I'd get at my favorite Italian restaurant.

My stomach contracts. "Who did you steal this from?" Not that I care. I'm totally eating it.

He slips me a fork and smiles. "I always keep a few extra meals in the fridge."

"Just in case a natural disaster strikes and you get stuck here?"

"Or in case I have to work late."

"Oh right. That." I prick a twisted noodle with the fork and bring it to my mouth, groaning at the garlic that pops on my tongue. "Oh my goodness. This is so good. Did you make it?"

"Yep." He dips a spoon into his dish, which looks like a potato soup of some sort. "My mom taught me how to cook before …"

Oh. It sounds like he's remembering something painful right now. Not knowing what to say, I place a bite of chicken into my mouth and wait for him to continue. The stars and moon are bright outside, streaming in through the windows, which must be why Connor didn't bother turning on the lights in the break room. It creates this cozy sort of atmosphere and also adds a kind of haunting sadness to the moment.

"She taught me when I was a teenager. I liked spending that time with her." He shifts in the hard plastic chair and shovels a bite of soup into his mouth.

I don't quite know what to make of this Connor. And in this moment, I realize I don't really know him at all—not the important stuff—and maybe I've judged him too harshly. Because any man who talks about his mom with such tenderness and nostalgia can't be all bad.

And I have the sudden urge to comfort him somehow—maybe even take his hand. But that's going just a bit too far. Still, I can offer words. I'm good at words. "My mom did her best to teach me the ropes of the kitchen, but I was a very bad student." My lips twitch at the memory. "One time I was cooking bacon on the stovetop and placed the hot skillet onto a potholder to take the cooked pieces off. But when I moved it back to the burner, I didn't realize that the potholder was stuck to the bottom."

"Uh oh."

"Yeah. It totally caught fire."

His eyes are wide as he laughs all staccato and throaty. "What happened?"

"As you may have ascertained"—I emphasize the word with a smile, a nod to his earlier *Webster* comment —"I am not the best in emergencies. So while most sane people would have simply removed the skillet and thrown some water from the sink over the potholder, I raced outside and grabbed the hose."

Now he's full-on laughing, and I love that he snorts all undignified-like. Somehow, it makes him slightly less demigod and more human. "You didn't."

"Oh yes, I did, sir." And I'm laughing too, my stomach hurting for a different reason now. "My mom still won't let me anywhere near her kitchen. After that, I was banished to helping my dad outside with the cows."

"Cows?"

"Oh. Yeah. I grew up on a dairy farm in Iowa."

"How have I worked with you for so long and never known that about you?" His spoon clinks on the glass container as he taps it against the edge. "In fact, how is this the first time we have ever really talked about something other than work?"

"I don't know." I chew my bottom lip, letting the silence between us hang there, almost a living thing. "I guess you've always preferred the company of everyone else in the office."

Great. That kind of sounded like I'm jealous.

Which I am *not*.

As if I can erase what I just said, I wave my hand quickly in the air. "What I mean is that you've always seemed more interested in talking to the other women …"

Nope. Not any better.

He sits back in his seat. "No, no. Go on." That cocky and amused grin he likes to wear is back.

It's always annoyed me before. But right now, in this ridiculous situation, I laugh. Like, full-on belly laugh. And he joins me. We sit there like a couple of fools laughing our heads off.

And for the first time since the earthquake scared the daylights out of me, I actually feel … okay. Calmer.

Like I'm not alone.

Because … I'm not.

I wipe the laugh tears from my eyes while he gathers the empty dishes and takes them to the sink, then turns back to me. "Time for some dessert." He reaches into his pocket, pulls loose his wallet, and heads to the vending machine. "What's your pleasure?"

I squint. "Are there any Reese's Pieces left?"

He whirls, jaw slack. "Is that your favorite or something?"

"One of them." His reaction is strange, like I just told him I'd seen a ghost. "Why?"

Shaking his head, he puts in money, makes his selection, and an orange box drops to the chute. "Last one." When he has it in hand, he comes back to the table and places the box between us.

"Aren't you going to get anything for yourself?"

"Oh, were you planning to eat the entire box?" he teases.

"Maybe," I tease back. Lifting the box, I peel at the cardboard top and the candy shakes inside like pinballs in a machine. When I've got it open, I drop several into my hand and scoop them all into my mouth, where flavor explodes and soothes. "Mmm. Peanut buttery goodness."

"Indeed." Connor takes a huge handful and sets them onto the table, then arranges them into groups by color—orange, yellow, brown. It's adorable. "You know, these are my favorite candy too." He glances up at me, winks. "Looks like we may have something in common after all."

"It's a good thing to have in common."

"It is, isn't it?" Wearing his usual mysterious smile, he picks up a yellow candy and sticks it in his mouth. "But unlike you, I like to savor them one at a time. No blending together of the colors for me."

"Are you serious? No way." I take another handful and shove them all in my mouth at once, sucking the outer shells away, chewing, and finally swallowing. "Besides, I don't taste a difference in the colors."

Now, his smile is different. Softer, somehow. "That's what she always said too."

I freeze. "Who?"

"My mom." He picks up an orange Reese's, turns it in his hand. "We used to watch the movie *E.T.* together. The one with the little alien who eats them? And we'd gorge ourselves until I felt sick."

He talks about her as if she's not around anymore. Like she left. Or died.

I clear my throat. "I remember that movie. It was one of my sister's favorites when we were kids." Talking about my sister always jabs me in the lungs, but ... I don't know. This time, the memory is only tinged with a ring of sadness instead of being consumed by it.

Almost as if, by sharing it with someone else—with Connor—it's a little easier to carry.

Which sounds kind of absurd, considering he doesn't even know my whole story and I don't know his.

Regardless, when our gazes connect in that moment, something inside of me shifts. And now I totally understand all of the story tropes in which characters bond after experiencing hardships together.

In which they fall for each other.

Because while I've always found Connor physically attractive, I'm actually starting to like him *as a person* too.

And that is obviously a very bad idea. After all, he's my competition for the associate publisher position. And he's ... Connor. He's still the biggest flirt I know, and I've always thought he was super shallow. Was I wrong? All this time? Because from where I'm sitting, he's actually been very level-headed and kind.

Almost ... sweet.

Before my thoughts can go ring-around-the-rosy another time, I push away the box of Reese's. "That was very good. Thanks." I fake a yawn and stretch my arms overhead. "I think it's about time for some shut-eye."

"Some shut-eye, huh?" He grins. "All right, Webster. Let's go."

And once again, I'm in his arms. This time, for the briefest second, I allow my head to find a pillow against his chest while he carries me back to my office. He sets me in my chair and I feel suddenly cold. I tug his suit jacket on again. If he thinks he's getting this back tonight, he has another thing coming.

Connor studies me for a minute, and a muscle in his jaw flexes. "Be right back." He spins and leaves, returning a minute later with a few blankets that I recognize from Justine's office. The woman always has a blanket across her lap while she works. I don't know if she's just perpetually cold-blooded or really likes the comfort a good blanket can provide. "I thought I could make a little bed on the floor."

Okay, forget I said he was "almost sweet." This is next-level. Which means that Connor Bryant is a total and complete sweetie pie.

Am I having a mental breakdown?

Stop it, Evie. No matter how sweet he is acting, you cannot fall for your totally hot co-worker. Because you are competitors. And you have to keep your eye on the prize, not on the guy who is suddenly more than you thought he was this morning.

Of course, maybe he hasn't changed at all. But my impression of him … that's what is shifting.

All of this internal pep talking has taken I-don't-know-how-long and Connor is still standing there with his arms full of blankets and waiting for me to stop being an idiot and answer him.

"Great idea. Thanks."

He studies me for a minute more, then nods. "No problem. There's plenty here, so you hopefully won't be too cold." After arranging them on the ground between the door and the desk, Connor grabs the door handle. "Sweet dreams, Evie."

Sweet dreams? Yeah, right.

I doubt I'll sleep a single wink tonight.

five

I DO SLEEP—AND, apparently, drool.

Something startles me awake and I sit up straight in my office chair. I blink as I swipe at the wetness pooling at the corners of my lips.

What time is it? I squint at the clock on my wall. Six-something. Makes sense considering that outside my window, there's just a tiny shimmer of light on the horizon. My computer is asleep, displaying my screen saver (which, yes, is totally Mr. Darcy staring straight at me … *le sigh*), and whew, it's cold in here. Maybe the heat doesn't come on overnight.

A shiver works its way through me and I pull the lapels of Connor's jacket tighter—and yes, inhale the still-there scent of him.

Memories of last night flood in. How I tried to get comfortable on my floor but couldn't sleep. How I came back to my desk and worked for a bit. How I then pulled out David and Stephanie's wedding invitation and, in my weakened and emotional state, cried.

Apparently after that, I conked out at my desk.

I rub a crick in my neck. Enough is enough. That invitation has already caused plenty of turmoil. Kayla said I should just throw it away and she's right. So I snag it once more—the stiff cream cardstock paper rough under my fingertips—and stand, surprised when my feet don't protest too loudly. Hallelujah. No more crawling for me.

I step gingerly around my desk and walk, ready to drop the invite inside the trash next to the door. But no. If I put it there, I'm liable to grab it out again—feeling guilty that I didn't RSVP.

Feeling guilty that I didn't go.

Which, honestly, is ridiculous. I know that it's ridiculous, and yet, I can't help how I feel. Because I should want the best for my ex and his future wife, right? I shouldn't be bitter. I should forgive and forget. Move on.

I have.

Have you?

With my annoyingly persistent subconscious's voice in my mind, I open my door and head slowly down the still-dim hallway toward the bathroom—because, hello, I have been holding it all night. Also, the trashcan in there is much deeper and I definitely won't go digging back through it once I regret tossing this sucker in.

As I reach the bathroom door, I hear music drifting from Connor's office. It's the pump-it-up kind that I imagine they play at the gym—wouldn't know since

I've never been to one. (Okay, I went once but immediately turned tail and ran when I caught sight of all the gorgeous women wearing sports bras and tiny shorts, their hair and makeup perfect. I, on the other hand, wore long basketball shorts and an oversized T-shirt, my hair pulled back in a ponytail and not a stitch of makeup on my face. How silly of me to think that one goes to the gym to … I don't know … work out.)

I expected Connor would be sleeping still, but if he can sleep through music like this, then color me impressed. Ever so quietly, I sneak up to his door, which is cracked an inch or two …

And it's totally enough space to see a shirtless Connor punching the air.

That's right, folks, he's just wearing gym shorts and doing some sort of boxing routine, shuffling his feet and jabbing one-two, one-two, and there's a tattoo snaking up his left bicep and, oh my goodness, his chest is every bit as chiseled as I'd always imagined.

Not that I spend a lot of time imagining it. Just … oh, shut up.

ANYWAY, I can't seem to pull my eyes off of him as he moves in time with the music. His hair is mussed in an adorable *I-just-rolled-out-of-bed* way and there's sweat dripping down his temples and running from his neck down the center of his chest toward his abs and I can't look away and now I'm sweating and KILL ME DEAD because he just caught me staring at him!

Whirling as fast as my injured feet will allow, I book it back down the hallway. But in my haste, the invitation flutters from my hands somewhere in between the bathroom door and Connor's office. Do I go back for it? Dare I risk him coming out of his office and catching me? If I go into the bathroom right now, I can deny the Peeping Tom incident. (Wait, what's the female equivalent of Tom? Tammy? Am I a Peeping Tammy? Oh, Lord!)

But before I can make a decision, Connor's music cuts out and his door opens all the way as he steps into the hallway. His smirk is bigger than the state of Texas. He totally knows I was checking him out.

This is bad. Really bad.

"Morning," I squeak, because what else can I say?

"Hi, there." He's got a shirt balled up in his hands and I will him with my mind to put it on—you know, so I can think like a rational human being instead of staring at him like some sort of pathetic woman who hasn't been so much as hugged by a man in more than two years.

Oh, wait. I totally *am* that woman. (And no, him carrying me yesterday didn't count as a hug.)

Groan, groan, groan on a stick.

"Um. So. Did you sleep well?" At this point, I'm clutching the frame of the bathroom door behind me. It's propping me up, thanks to my gelatin-for-legs.

"I did. You?"

"Mmm hmm." Finally, my eyes meet his gaze.

He laughs and tugs the quick-dry shirt over his head.

Oh, thank goodness. The tension in my shoulders eases. I clear my throat. "My feet are feeling better." As if it wasn't obvious.

His features soften. "I'm glad to hear that. We should

take a look and make sure they're not infected or anything."

"I'm sure they're—"

"Fine. I know." He holds up his hands in surrender. "But it'll make me feel better to check."

Oh. I bite my lip and nod. "Yeah, all right." Man, this is awkward. What would a normal person say right now? Food. Food is always a safe topic, right? "Are you hungry? I figured I'd scrounge up some breakfast from the vending machine. My treat since you fed us last night. I think I saw some Pop-Tarts in there." I pause, straighten, then fidget with the sleeves of his jacket. I should probably give this back to him.

Not yet.

"Breakfast of champions." His eyes twinkle. "That sounds good. Just give me time to get cleaned up. Guess it'll be a good old-fashioned sponge bath in the bathroom sink for me today."

Don't you dare picture that, Evie Denmark.

"Great!" I blurt out. "Well, I'll let you get to it, then."

"Okay." And just before he goes back into his office, his gaze flickers to the ground.

To the invitation.

No!

He starts toward it and I scramble. "Oh! That's mine, actually."

But Connor gets there first. He squats, picks it up, and hands it to me. "Here you go."

I clutch it to my chest as if I'm thirteen and it's my diary. "Thank you."

"Am I allowed to ask why you're walking the halls with a wedding invitation?"

Yeah, why would any sane person be doing that? Maybe the truth is the least crazy thing I can say. "I'm throwing it away."

He doesn't reply, just stands there, watching me. Waiting … for what?

I lick my lips. "The thing is … the invite is for the wedding of my ex-boyfriend and his fiancée, who used to be one of my best friends."

"And they invited you? Were they trying to be jerks or something?"

My finger trails the edge of the fancy paper, over the raised bumps and grooves. "We're kind of still in touch."

"Like, you're friends?"

"Maybe." I cringe at the crackle in my voice, so I rush on. "I mean, not really, but we've gotten together over the years to catch up once or twice." Or six times, but who's counting?

And those were the most miserable memories of my life—sitting at a restaurant on one side of a booth, the two of them on the other, David's arm slung around Stephanie's shoulders like it used to be around mine. Each time, I came home and cried, and Kayla scolded me for going in the first place.

But I couldn't say no to Stephanie's invitations to dinner, because … I don't know. It's like I had to prove that I was the bigger person. Or maybe I can't stand the idea that there's someone out there I'm at odds with.

"Were you and your ex serious?"

I know what he's implying—that maybe this isn't a big deal. Maybe we only dated for a short amount of time and I gave Steph my blessing to date my ex.

A breath shudders in, out. "We dated for three years."

"Wow, I'm sorry."

I kick at an invisible pebble on the carpet and shrug, like it's no big deal. "Apparently he spent half of those pining after my friend who finally agreed to date him if he dumped me." Ugh, why did I tell him that? It will only add to his pathetic image of me—the dowdy editor who is not only a glutton for punishment, but unlovable to boot.

"So are you going to go to the wedding?"

I sigh. Because even though I'm throwing the invitation away, I know myself. And in five weeks, on April second, I will most likely be sitting in the audience at David and Stephanie's wedding. "Probably."

"Like … alone? Or is your boyfriend going with you?"

That makes me laugh—one of those short, disbelieving laughs. "You think I have a boyfriend?"

A hand runs over his stubble, which is more pronounced today. "I didn't know."

"Well, I don't." I lift my chin ever so slightly. "I'm focusing on my career right now." Yeah, that's right. It's my choice. Because I love my job and want to go even further at this company.

My lack of a romantic relationship has nothing to do with the fact I'm terrified to fall in love again with someone who doesn't love me back.

Nope. Not at all.

"But you've at least got a hot date lined up, right?"

My face flushes. "My roommate Kayla will probably come with me."

He gently takes the invitation from my hands, and I willingly let it go. Staring at it, he shakes his head. "You're a much bigger person than me. Not sure I'd be able to attend an ex's wedding—especially without a proper date. Don't you want to make him jealous?"

Is he kidding? Nothing I do will ever make David jealous. Why would it? To him, I'm not worthy of notice —not when someone like Stephanie is around.

And yeah, it would feel good to somehow prove to them both that I've moved on, that their actions don't affect me one bit.

But short of paying someone to date me, I'm not seeing that as an option. "I don't really want to talk about this anymore."

He takes one step closer, and I can smell the salty sweat on his skin. And there's a whiff of some sort of body spray too. "Sorry if I upset you. I just think you should show that jerk what he's missing."

I stiffen at his words, at the smile—and tease?—in them. Is he *flirting* with me? No, no. He's just being nice again for some reason.

Nevertheless, his words make me equal parts want to laugh and cry. I point at myself. "And just what would that be? My luscious head of greasy hair? Or maybe the stained grandma clothing? Or, I know!" I waggle my eyebrows as I lift my skirt an inch to show off my right knee. "Would it be the milky white skin? Or—"

"Come on, Evie. You don't give yourself enough credit." And then he's staring at me, and for a moment, it's almost as if he's seeing me … really seeing me … for the first time. But then he steps back, gives a short laugh, and runs his hand through his hair. "But for real. You should find yourself a handsome date and wear something hot and dance all night and give Mr. Atkinson an eyeful of what he gave up."

The tiny hairs on my arms rise at the mental image of me doing exactly what Connor is suggesting. And sure, Kayla could stuff me into a suitable outfit, do my hair and makeup, the whole nine yards. Maybe I could even take dancing lessons so I don't look like a total idiot on the dance floor.

But there's one little problem with his suggestion. (Hint: It's not a little problem. It's a very big one.)

I drop a hand to my hip. "We don't all have a thousand potential lovers waiting in the wings."

At that he grins again. "You don't need a thousand. You just need one."

I tap my chin like I'm considering alllll of my options —what a laugh. "Can he be fictional?" Because other than Sir Isaac, I've got nada.

"You don't need someone fictional. You've got me."

"You?" I sputter. Did he just say …? He's joking. He has to be.

"Yeah, me."

What. Is. Happening? My heart thrums against my chest.

He lifts a hand and gently presses my chin upward to close my gawking, open mouth. "Why not?"

Why not? I know plenty of *why nots*, starting with the fact that we're competing for the same job. But the real question isn't why not … it's why?

I push his hand away, and his fingers leave my skin warm and tingly. Still, I narrow my gaze at him. Because after working together for a decade and never once having a personal conversation, this has to be a joke. What is this guy playing at? "Why would you do that for me? And what would you want in return?"

"I'd do it because I'm a really nice guy." He shoves his hands into the pockets of his shorts, so casual—as if his suggestion that we go on a date together hasn't just rocked my entire world and everything I thought I knew about him. "As for what I want in return, I can think of one thing …"

And the way he trails off lets me know exactly what that one thing is.

I hold back the urge to slap him, but I can't keep my eyes from flashing my rage. "Seriously, Connor? What happened to being a nice guy?"

"What?" His face morphs from amusement to confusion to something twisted like horror. "No, Evie! How could you think that's what I was talking about?"

"With your reputation, what else *would* I think, Connor?" But as we stand there, eyes locked, I start to doubt myself. "It's just that you're always flirting …" Nope, that's not better. I expire a steady breath. "Sorry."

But it's too late for an apology because something in

his gaze closes off. "No worries." He holds out the invitation for me a final time.

I take it, my fingers trembling. Before I can open my mouth to apologize again, he steps away. "I think I'm going to eat breakfast in my office. There's something I forgot I need to do before Monday. Might as well use this time to get it done."

He turns and strides into his office, and this time, the door shuts all the way.

For the next few hours, I try to work.

But my mind can't handle the intricacies of Regency England at the moment—I'm stuck in the present, where a very attractive man has offered to be my date to my ex's wedding.

Where I was a jerk and made assumptions about him and his motives.

Still, my mind keeps circling back to what he *was* talking about. What would Connor want in return for going with me?

Finally, I can't stand it anymore. I hobble into the break room, buy a load of snacks, and haul them into Connor's office. He's sitting behind his desk, staring at the computer screen. When I walk in, his gaze clouds and a frown appears. "What can I help you with, Ms. Denmark?"

Oh, we're back to the formalities, are we? "Hi,

Connor." I step forward. All of my visits to his office have been fairly brief in the past—and this one might be too, depending on how he reacts to me. His walls are littered with awards for various sales and marketing campaigns, and the only thing on his pristine desk other than his computer, lamp, and pen holder is a photo of him with a large golden retriever.

He lifts an eyebrow at me. Once again he's wearing his dress shirt. It's no longer crisp, but the sleeves are rolled up to his elbows, revealing tan, corded arms that lead to powerful, slightly calloused fingers. I imagine those hands wrapped around my waist, holding me close on the dance floor at David's wedding.

Delicious shivers wind up my spine.

Why did I come in here again? Oh, yeah. I dump my armful of goodies onto his desk and wave my hand at the pile, which includes a bag of pretzels, Skittles, a Clif bar, and chocolate in various forms. "I thought you might be hungry."

He takes me in with his darkened brow, and I have no idea what he's thinking. Internally, I'm just begging him to crack a smile, make a joke. But in one quick motion, he sweeps the snacks out of his way and turns back to the computer. "I'm not."

I groan and flop into the chair opposite of him. "Come on, Connor. I'm really sorry for what I said." Except … it was the truth. The part about his reputation, anyway. But that's neither here nor there. "And I'm here to ask what it is you *would* want in exchange for going with me to David and Stephanie's wedding."

Because I've decided that I very much would like

that. It's not as if I want David back—not after the way he discarded me like a used tissue—but I love the idea of proving to everyone (David, his family, and all of the friends I stopped hanging out with when they supported Stephanie instead of me) that I've moved on.

Proving that I'm not falling apart.

And that's honestly the truth—I'm *not* falling apart. Not anymore. I've got a job I love, roommates I adore, and parents who need me. But unfortunately, none of those facts will be as effective at convincing my former social circle of my transcendence as if I show up with a hunky man on my arm.

Speaking of said hunky man, Connor is being really quiet. Maybe he's rethinking our deal—not that we have a deal. Yet.

But my itching fingertips are proof of just how much I hope we can come to one. And it has nothing to do with the fact I'd get to go on a date with him.

NOTHING.

Because I. Don't. Like. Him.

And he definitely doesn't like me.

After what feels like hours, he swivels in his chair to face me. Snatching up a pen from his desk, he clicks the end a few times. "I thought you already knew what I wanted."

"You said I was wrong." I want so badly to look away, but I also want him to know this isn't a game to me. "I'm giving you a chance to explain."

"How *magnanimous* of you." His lips twitch.

I exhale a relieved breath. If he's almost smiling, then we're going to be fine. "Who's Webster now?"

"Touché." He sets down the pen and opens his desk drawer, pulling out a large stack of papers that are secured together with a thick rubber band. Connor gazes at it fondly, tapping his fingers along the top before nodding and scooting it across the desk toward me. "I want your help with this."

"What is it?" But before he can answer, I'm reading the top typed paper—*The Girl Next Door* by Bryant Purcell. My nose crinkles. "A book?"

I turn to the first page and read a few paragraphs. Then I flip farther in, read more. It appears to be a contemporary romance, and from what I can tell, the author is very talented. Obviously I've only read a little, but I've learned to trust my instincts over the years. And my instincts are telling me that this is the kind of book that will make me grab one of those chocolate bars on Connor's desk, lock myself in my office, and devour the whole thing in one sitting (the chocolate and the book).

"So what's the favor? Did you discover this author and want me to consider contracting him? Because you know we only do historicals." Maybe this Bryant guy is a friend.

Wait. Bryant.

As in … Connor Bryant?

I glance up and flinch at the intensity of his stare. When our gazes collide, he looks away and fiddles with his computer mouse.

"Is this yours?"

The tips of his ears look red, but it's kind of dim in here—the lights are still at half power and it's a cloudy morning in San Diego, surprise, surprise—so I could be mistaken. But I don't miss the subtle nod he gives or the way he coughs.

Almost like he's embarrassed.

But plenty of guys write romance novels. We publish quite a few. There's nothing to be ashamed about. "Hey, this is really good."

He whips his head around. "It is?"

"Yeah." I bite the inside of my cheek to keep from grinning. Is this the first time I've ever seen Connor look unsure about something? It's kind of adorable. "How many books have you written?"

He scratches the back of his neck. "A few. But this is the first one I've felt is decent enough to show to someone else."

And I get to be that lucky someone. "So how can I help?"

"You're obviously brilliant when it comes to editing."

His words of praise shouldn't make me blush, but they do. "Thank you."

"Just speaking the truth." Connor points to the manuscript. "Could you just … I don't know. Read it and give me your thoughts?"

"Sure. Absolutely." I run my fingertip along the smooth rubber of the band holding the papers together. "And you'd really go with me to the wedding?"

"If you'd still want me to … despite my reputation."

I cringe. "Connor, listen—"

"It's fine, Evie. Don't think anything more about it. I know what people say about me." His full-on Cheshire grin returns as he stands and rounds the desk, leaning back against it—right in front of me. "It's hard being so popular, but someone's got to do it."

There he goes again, making me laugh at his bravado. "Oh, brother." But then I sober up quickly, because I need something clarified. "Just to be sure we're on the same page, you'll be my date to the wedding. What …" I fidget with my skirt. "What would that look like?"

"Whatever you're comfortable with. I could just be a stand-in date. Arm candy, if you will." We both laugh.

Then he pauses, cocks his head, studies me, almost like he's unsure again. "Or we could pretend like we're, you know, together. Just for show, of course."

"Of course." It's ridiculous that disappointment pinches that spot between my lungs. "And you wouldn't mind? Pretending, I mean?"

"No way. I have absolutely no qualms with putting that ex of yours in his place."

Even though there's a flutter of a warning in my chest—lying of any sort twists me up inside—I appreciate the strength of his dislike for David simply because he's hurt me.

And yeah, gotta admit I don't hate the idea of pretending for a night that a man like Connor Bryant—who could pretty much have any woman he wants—is interested in *me*.

"Okay." I pause, considering. He's probably going to say no to my next question. Then again, he's asking me to invest a lot of hours of my time in reading and critiquing his manuscript, so I feel like I have the right to ask him to commit the same number of hours—probably fewer, actually. "Do you think we could tack on the wedding shower as part of the deal too? Apparently it's a couples thing."

Wait, what am I thinking? Pretending to date me at one event is one thing. To ask him to spend a few extra hours pretending … I just don't want to push my luck. So I plow on before he can answer. "You know what? Never mind. That's too much to ask."

And wow, I've overstayed my welcome, haven't I? I tap the manuscript in my lap. "When do you need this back by?"

It isn't until I stand that I realize how close we are—just inches from each other. I can smell the soap he must have used to wash up in the bathroom earlier. Can hear my blood whooshing in my veins (it's super loud and I really hope he can't also hear it). Can feel the intensity he's capable of, pulsing off of him.

Can see his Adam's apple bob.

Can almost mentally taste his lips—and if I were to simply lean forward a single inch, I'd be able to taste them in real life too.

For a moment, his pupils seem to dilate as he watches me. "Evie."

I'm mesmerized by the husky vibrations in his voice. "Yeah?"

"It's not too much to ask. I'm happy to go to the shower and the wedding with you."

"Are you sure? Because the shower is next weekend."

Then Connor's hand slides up my lower arm, his touch feather soft, catching my elbow and continuing on to my shoulder—all the while, leaving a trail of wildfire in its wake. Then his fingers land on my cheek, the gentle pressure sending heavenly tingles throughout my whole body. "I'm sure, Webster. And as for the manuscript, get to it when you can. No rush."

Before I can squeak out a reply, there's a strange persistent knock coming from the front of our office.

Connor's eyebrows knit together and then lift. "Come on." He grabs my hand and pulls me toward the door. "I think we're being rescued."

six

. . .

"I CAN'T BELIEVE you were stuck overnight with the hottest man you know and didn't so much as kiss his cheek!" Kayla groans and collapses on our couch dramatically.

"I knew you'd be disappointed in me." It's been an hour since Kayla picked me up at the hospital, where the rescue crew insisted Connor and I go to get checked out (my feet should be healed in a few days, thank goodness!). Now that I'm freshly showered and finally in my comfy pajamas, I've just finished giving Kayla a play-by-play of my time with Connor. Of course, she's haranguing me about my lack of romantic prowess, but what's new?

I sink into the living room's funky patchwork wing-back chair. Alexis, who owns the house we live in, has decorated all the common areas in bright colors. There are magenta curtains on the windows, lime green throw pillows on the royal blue couch, and yellow-accented abstract art on the walls.

I shouldn't be surprised. Alexis herself is a walking color palette. We never know what color her hair is going to be.

"What kind of romance reader are you, anyway? I mean, you couldn't have a better meet-cute than him putting his arms around you and giving you his jacket."

She has a point, but there's one thing she's forgetting. "That's exactly it, Kay. I'm a *reader*. I spend my days living vicariously through other people—and fictional ones at that." I tug my long hair back into a ponytail, using the rubber band around my wrist to secure it. "The romance doesn't usually happen to *me*."

"Or maybe it does, and you just choose to ignore it." Kayla tosses the throw pillow at me. "When I picked you up tonight, I saw your face when Mr. Hottie hugged you goodbye. You seriously looked like you'd just eaten your mom's Seven Minutes in Heaven Chocolate Cheesecake."

I smile—at the silly name my mother gave her "famous" dessert, not realizing that she'd basically named it after a horny kissing game played by teenagers —but then sober up when my brain comprehends Kayla's meaning. "Yes, as we've established, he's very attractive." And yeah, maybe I sank into his embrace like a rock in water. "But it was just a hug."

"No way. It's more than that." Kayla pins me with what I affectionately call her gotcha gaze. "You like him. He likes you. Why else would he suggest going on a date?"

I fiddle with the tassels of the pillow, which remind me of tiny white pompoms. "Because he needs an editor for his manuscript, and he thinks nothing of going on a date. He goes on dates all the time. They're nothing special to him."

"So why has he never asked *you* on a date before now? If it's no big deal and he's literally gone out with almost every other female in that office?"

"He just doesn't see me like that." Not that I can blame him.

"Stop it." Kayla sits up and points a finger at me. "You're doing that thing again."

"No, I'm not." I hesitate. "What thing?"

"That thing where you doubt what a freaking catch you are."

"Oh. Well." Now I'm gripping the pillow to my chest, so tight that if it were a balloon, it would pop and scatter fake fluff everywhere. "I'm just being realistic. I'm not his type."

"So his type isn't gorgeous, brilliant, and kind?"

"Ha." I swallow, my throat full of cotton balls. "Maybe he's just not my type."

"Well, that's just ridiculous because tall, dark, and luscious with muscles for days is everyone's type."

"Exactly. I can't compete with all of those other women." I rest my chin on the top of the pillow. "Not that I want to."

"You're just scared, Evie. How many times do I have to remind you?" Her eyes soften. "Not all men are jerks like David. Someone someday is going to see you— really see you—and love every inch of what he sees."

Aw, geez. I look away, toward the sixty-inch television mounted to the wall. On the mantel, Alexis has placed a few framed photos—one of her and her younger sister Kennedy, who lives in San Francisco, and another of all of us. Kayla and I have only known each other since we both answered the ad Alexis placed looking for housemates seven years ago. There were two other women who lived here for a while, but it wasn't until Shelby and Lauren moved in three years ago that our group felt complete. And now, they're my family away from home.

I don't want to have to leave them. Moving back to Iowa would be …

Don't think about that. You're going to get that promotion.

You have to.

Shaking free of the thought, I return my attention to Kayla. "I love your confidence in me."

"I just wish you'd be as confident in yourself."

My friend just doesn't get it, but that's because two people probably couldn't be more opposite. After all, *confident* is her middle name. She's hot stuff and wicked smart, and she knows it. Not that she's arrogant. There's a fine line between arrogance and confidence, but she walks that line with grace.

My phone pings on the side table next to me. I pick it up and blink as I read the screen.

Connor: *So what's the dress code for this bridal shower thing, anyway? Formal? Super casual? Athleisure-wear? *smiley face wink* What are you planning to wear?*

I've had his number in my phone contacts for a long time—Lisa encouraged us to exchange info when we were working together on a big project years ago—but this is the first time he's ever texted me.

Ever.

Which is why I'm staring dumbly at the screen when Kayla asks who it's from. When I don't answer, she jumps off the couch and yanks the phone from my grip. Her eyebrows go up and her jaw drops. "Girl! He's into you."

My stomach drops at her proclamation. "He is not."

I can't deny that Kayla does seem to have an uncanny ability to predict which couples will get together, which will last, and which will break up after a few months (she told me after David and I broke up that she knew it was going to happen). But she's wrong about this.

Scooting to the edge of my chair, I hold out my hand. "Kindly return my phone now."

"Not until we figure out the perfect answer." Kayla taps her chin. "Oh, I know!" Her fingers fly across the screen.

I lunge for her, but she's too quick for me. "Kay!"

"There! All done." Her singsong tone grates against my ears as she shoves the phone back into my hands.

Evie: *Wouldn't you like to know. *Smiling kissy face**

"Kayla!" Tossing my phone onto the couch as if it's burned me, I have the very strong urge to murder my best friend. "Now he thinks I'm flirting with him."

"And why shouldn't you? He's gorgeous. Single. An

author—which would not turn me on in the slightest, but you? Hello!" She's ticking off Connor's attributes one by one, and I can't help but be in silent agreement with each of her points. "And, from what you've told me, he's sweet too. He took care of you when you were scared, fed you when you were hangry, and bandaged your wounds. If I were you, I'd be flirting it up allllll day."

I bury my face in my hands. "I have no idea how to flirt!"

"All you have to do is say the word and I will teach you."

My head pops back up. She's not joking. "Kay, I love you, but even you can't teach this old dog that new trick. I'd be like Albert Brennaman in *Hitch*." (And in case you're not up on your romcom knowledge from the early 2000s, that's the super awkward guy who hires a dating coach because he wants to win the affections of a woman way out of his league—the guy who drops mustard on his pants, dances like a freak show, and has to pull out his inhaler before kissing her. And yes, he ends up getting the girl, but that's beside the point.)

But my bestie rubs her hands together, a semi-wicked grin on her face. "Oh, my young *padawan*. You have no idea who you are dealing with."

"Padawan?"

"It's a *Star Wars* reference." Oh, right. She may be sophisticated and chic, but Kayla is also a closet nerd. (No one knows this but me, and she will murder me if she finds out I ever told.) "It's like an apprentice. A student. You will be my student, and I will teach you how to flirt."

I laugh—loudly. Because the idea, it's just … well, silly. Ludicrous. Farcical. (What? Connor doesn't call me Webster for nothing.) "Even if you could somehow achieve this miraculous feat, I can't go flirting with Connor."

"And just why not?"

"I've already told you. He's my co-worker, and we're competing for the same job. Flirting with him could just get … complicated."

"Or it could be the perfect opportunity for you to get back on the horse without any sort of serious commitment."

"What do you mean?"

My friend sighs. "You're never going to be a serial dater, Evie. And I love that about you. But David really rocked your confidence. So maybe Connor—someone who doesn't seem to take dating all that seriously—is the perfect guy to practice your skills on. There's no expectation for a relationship. Just fun."

Oh. Hmmm. Maybe her idea has merit. But before I can really consider it, I whisk it from my mind. "I have to stay focused on getting the promotion."

"Flirting is all about having confidence in what you have to offer. Have you ever thought that maybe showing more confidence in yourself could help you get the promotion?" Kayla cocks her head. "Your boss knows you're a hard worker, but you think Connor will get the job because of how well he can schmooze. Where do you think that schmooze-y talent comes from? His self-confidence."

"I guess I never thought of it like that."

"So. Will you let me give you some confidence lessons?"

My stomach flips at the absurd notion. "What all would that entail?"

"Other than some more generalized confidence coaching, I'll give you lessons in the art of flirting and how to deal with different situations on a date." She looks me up and down, lips pursed. "And, if you're okay with it, I'll also give you a bit of a makeover."

It hits me in the gut, the idea that even my bestie wants to change me. "I don't know."

"And before you go thinking that it's because you're not good enough as you are, the purpose of the makeover wouldn't be to change or 'improve' you, because there's nothing that needs improvement."

"So you're not going to put me in leather pants like Sandy at the end of *Grease*?"

She winks at me. "I think Connor would probably like that, but no."

Ha. "That's good, because I'm pretty sure those would only look good on you."

"I do have the butt for them, but you're delusional if you think I'd ever wear them." Then she gets all serious on me again, grabbing my hand. "Evie, let me do this for you. Let me help you find yourself again—love yourself again. Because I love you and so does everyone who really knows you." She grins. "And, if my instincts are right, Connor is starting to as well. He might even already be there."

"Now who's delusional?" I squeeze her hand and let go when my phone pings again from the couch. Rushing over, I pick it up and read the message.

Connor: *I'll show you mine if you show me yours.*

Oh. My. Holy. Freaking. Cow. I turn the phone around to show Kayla, wide-eyed. "What have you done? There's no way I can go on a date with him now. He probably thinks I want to hook up or something."

She reads the message and laughs the exotic laugh of a confident Superwoman. "Maybe you should."

I pinch her in the side and she twists away from me, cackling some more. Another message rolls in. She grabs the phone, squints at it, and rolls her eyes. "You've got nothing to worry about, girl."

"What do you mean?" Snatching the phone back, I look at the string of messages and breathe a sigh of relief.

Connor: *I meant my outfit. Get your mind out of the gutter, Webster. *laugh-crying smiley face**

Connor: *For real though, let me know the dress code when you get a sec. I need time to perfect my look. It's not like I just roll out of bed looking this gorgeous.*

Oh, that man. I smirk, slumping back onto the couch. "He's so good at this. Flirting is like breathing to him."

Kayla tosses her hair over her shoulder and pulls me to my feet once more. "Once I'm finished with you, you'll be teaching Connor Bryant a thing or two." Something flashes in her eyes. She likes the challenge, I can tell. "Are you in?"

Biting my lip, I consider everything she's said. I'll do anything to get that promotion—even let my friend dress me up. And, maybe the process will help me become a bit less awkward when it comes to the male species.

So before I can run back to my room, I give a firm nod. "All right. Let's do this."

seven

· · ·

I'M GOING to hurl all over Kayla's Louboutins.

And possibly fall on my face because I never, I repeat NEVER, in my life have worn anything above a one-inch heel. And these puppies are spiked sky high. Pretty sure they're going to be the death of me.

"I feel ridiculous." I stare at myself in the full-length mirror in our bedroom, at the transformation my best friend has wrought. I'm no longer librarian Evie, but sexy-date-night Evie—and I don't recognize this woman. My hair is freshly cut to just below my shoulders, highlighted, and curled. It looks impossibly soft and I actually really like how it catches the light now, much more than my drab brown color before.

But my outfit, well, that's another matter.

The olive-colored ruched dress hovers mid-thigh and features a deep V neckline (I'm tempted to safety pin the sides together, but Kayla would kill me) that I'm fairly certain would make my mother faint outright. Although

I can't deny that Kayla found just the right piece of clothing to show off my curves and legs to my best advantage, I can't help but feel … exposed.

Like I'm trying too hard.

"Well, you don't *look* ridiculous." Kayla is in the walk-in closet, searching her jewelry box for a necklace she claims will complete the ensemble. She emerges, triumphant and clutching a sparkly choker-style necklace with a long drop chain.

I hold back a groan as she places it around my neck. "Isn't it going to draw the eyes, um, downward?"

"That's kind of the point. Kidding, kidding." Kayla steps back to scrutinize her work. "It's the perfect complement."

She says she's kidding, but I'm not so sure.

That's it. I swivel on my heel and nearly fall over. After clutching the top of my dresser for support, I hightail it to the closet and pull a sweater off its hanger. But before I can wrap it around my body, my supposed friend snatches it from me. "Evie Denmark, you are not going to cover yourself up. Not tonight."

"But—"

"Do you remember nothing I've taught you this week?" Kayla holds the sweater far away from me and I'm tempted to lunge for it, but I'm pretty sure I'd break the heel off her pumps. And on my salary, there's no way I can afford to replace the designer shoes.

"Yes, I remember." How could I not? I've spent every evening for the last six days getting "confidence lessons" drilled into me, as well as some "Dating 101" tips and role-play exercises in which Kayla pretended to be Connor. (Can you say *awkward*???)

Except for a few moments that left us rolling with laughter, Kayla's been a drill sergeant, whipping me into shape. And guess what? I'm really, really out of shape when it comes to dating.

Not sure I was ever *in* shape to begin with.

Thus, the roiling in my stomach and the pressing need to vomit up the crackers I managed to eat a few hours ago before getting dressed for the couple shower that starts in thirty minutes. Connor will be here soon and he's going to take one look at me and know—know! —that I am an imposter.

He will also know that I like him.

Gah! I don't want to, but he's made it impossible with his cute little texts all week long. Because everyone is working from home until our office building is inhabitable again, I haven't had to see him in person. (Thankfully, Kayla's initial assessment about the earthquake was right. Most of San Diego fared well enough, and the injury count was low—a real miracle, actually.)

Unfortunately, I've now got a week's worth of Kayla's sayings volleying around in my head. (Things like, "Maintain eye contact!" "Don't slouch!" "Remember to ask questions!" "Stop fidgeting—it shows your lack of confidence.")

So who knows how awkward tonight is going to be.

My bestie can obviously sense my nerves, because she takes one final look at me, fluffs my hair, and pulls me into a quick hug. "You've got this, Evie. You are the total package. Everyone else knows it. Now you go and believe it too."

All she needs are some pompoms and she'll be the best cheerleader ever. I smile at her faith in me and salute. "I'll do my best, Coach."

She claps her hands in quick succession. The drill sergeant is back. "I want you to spend two minutes in a power pose to get those hormones flowing. Connor will be here soon."

My muscles twitch at the thought. What is he going to think of this get-up? "Yes, ma'am."

I still feel silly every time I do this, but I stand with my feet apart and place my hands on my hips, my chest puffed out. I'm like Wonder Woman without the cape (and the whip). Kayla made me watch this TED Talk about how our perception of ourselves can be changed by our nonverbal actions. Apparently when we feel powerless, we tend to make ourselves smaller. When we feel powerful, we make ourselves bigger. The speaker thought that by practicing these "power poses" before an important interaction, we can actually change our hormonal reaction to the situation.

It was fascinating. And I guess we will see if it works tonight.

The doorbell rings. Kayla holds up a finger. "I'll get that. You still have one more minute in that pose. Then I want you to walk out of this room like the sexy, brilliant woman you are."

"Okay," I mumble.

"I can't hear you!" Her annoying singsong tone is

back and I kind of want to stuff a pillow in her face to muffle it.

But obviously, I don't. "Okay!" I chirp out as enthusiastically as I can.

"That's the spirit." My friend winks and disappears.

A second later our housemate Lauren pokes her head inside the room. She's wearing her usual fare—cute little cycling shorts (she teaches spin classes) and a tight tank that show off her extremely toned body—and her eyes widen as she emits a low whistle. "Where did those boobs come from?"

Lauren turns her head down the hallway. "Shelbs, Alexis, come here! Quick, before Evie changes her mind and stays in tonight." She must see the deer-in-the-headlights look I'm sure is written all over my face.

But seriously, what *am* I thinking?

I drop my hands from the power pose and look frantically around for the sweater Kayla stole from me. There, on her bed! I dive for it but the stupid heels (the death of me, I tell you!) catch on the carpet and I plummet face-first onto the bed with a squeal. Somehow the momentum pushes my legs clear over my head and I land with a thud in a heap on the ground.

Ow. Ooooow.

There's a commotion at the door, and before I can react, a pair of strong arms is lifting me from the ground —and it kind of feels like déjà vu as I turn to find myself in Connor's embrace. "Um, hi."

He's wearing a suit and tie like usual, and he smells incredible—also as usual. His grin is magnetic as his hands grip me fast. "We have to stop meeting like this."

And then I giggle like a deranged hyena. That's how it sounds to my ears, anyway.

Oh, goodness.

I clear my throat and straighten, stepping away from him, my legs as shaky as a newborn giraffe's.

The effect is worsened when his jaw drops at the full sight of me.

"I know." My cheeks burn as I quickly double check whether my fall dislodged any of my assets (ahem), but thankfully the girls are tucked right where they're supposed to be. "I went a little overboard with the dress, huh?" With trembling fingers, I adjust the necklace, which has moved slightly askew, then run my hands down my thighs to smooth out the dress.

As Connor's eyes follow my hands, his silence speaks volumes—he knows, just like I do, that I can't pull off this outfit. I can't be all the things Kayla wants me to be tonight. Honestly, it would probably be best to call off this whole night, let Connor off the hook. I can't stand the embarrassment anymore, so I pivot toward the door, stooping to pick up the sweater that started this mess in the first place.

But then I catch Kayla's eye—and the eyes of all my other housemates, who are totally spying on Connor and me from the doorway. The rest of them whirl and leave, but Kayla stays and shoos me back toward Connor with a narrowed glare. She puffs out her chest and mouths "power pose" before leaving Connor and me alone.

I stop and close my eyes for a moment. Right. Before I go any farther, I lift my shoulders, drop the sweater, and turn back to Connor—who is still staring at me. But who cares what he thinks, right?

Tonight, I get to be someone else. And I'm going to enjoy it.

So I hold out my hand and plaster on a huge old fake-it-till-I-make-it grin. "Ready?"

He blinks and furrows his brow, then steps forward to take my hand. "Ready."

"Great." I turn to go, but he holds me fast. I look back at him, a question in my eyes.

"You didn't go overboard. You look perfect."

Surely he just means I look perfect to accomplish my task for the night—make David jealous. Or rather, prove to him and Stephanie that I've moved on.

And there's no better way to do that than to show up with Connor on my arm, looking like a million bucks and practicing those confidence-slash-flirting skills Kayla's been pounding into my brain all week.

"Thank you." I say it with a smile and way more confidence than I feel. Squeezing his hand, I let go and grab my purse off the dresser. "Let's do this, shall we?"

By the time Connor and I pull up in front of the La Jolla country club where the couple shower is being held, all of that bravado is gone. I'm going to need to power pose myself to death tonight if I'm to survive.

The whole way over, Connor has been fairly quiet.

We've mostly talked about work, and a little bit about his manuscript, which I'm reading for the second time through (not that the last week provided a lot of free time). Overall, it's really good, but there are definitely some things we need to talk about if he wants to get it published. We've set a tentative time a week from now to get together and chat about my notes.

Connor exits his Lexus and walks around to my side of the car, opening the door and lending me his hand. Every time he touches me, it's like ice shoots into my veins—and in this particular moment, I can't help but think of that part in the 2005 version of *Pride & Prejudice* (which is inferior in every way, except for this one scene) when Mr. Darcy helps Lizzie into the carriage and then flexes his hand afterward.

Not that Connor's hand is flexing, but mine sure is when he lets go.

He tosses the keys to the valet and gives me his arm. I can feel his muscles bulging underneath his crisp blue jacket as we walk into the country club. When he asks the concierge where the shower is, they don't point us to a ballroom like I expect, but toward the beach instead. We walk through the high-ceilinged lobby, which features a large diamond-encrusted chandelier and cream leather furniture, and take a path out the back doors through a throng of overhanging trees. Eventually the trail opens up and meets the sand of the country club's private beach.

My breath whooshes as I take in the gorgeous landscape—the darkening sky like a blanket inlaid with a thousand glittering jewels, the faint outline of the coast to the south. People mingle on the sand, where about ten driftwood tables are draped with gauzy white-and-blue runners. Twinkle lights are strung from poles surrounding the tables, which are decorated with what looks like hurricane vases, candles, and seashells. Soft music plays from some invisible speakers, and the melody of the sea contributes to the peaceful harmony.

Connor whistles beside me. "Are all bridal showers this swanky?"

I'd forgotten how rich Stephanie's dad is. And this is only the shower—no doubt the wedding itself will be even fancier. "Definitely not." That's all I can say, because *of course* David would rather marry into this family than mine. Although, Stephanie's parents—especially her mom—were super overbearing the one time I met them. So actually, it's David's loss, because my family is amazing.

But that doesn't mean I'm not intimidated by the scene unfolding before us.

"Look." Connor points to our right, where a country club employee is standing behind a podium of sorts. A sign that reads Shoe Check is hanging across the front. "Is that like a coat check, but for shoes?"

"Apparently." I point to a woman who is tugging off her heels, laughing as she chats with her date and follows him toward the tables.

"All right then." Without hesitation, Connor plops onto the sand and pulls off his socks and dress shoes. He looks up at me, then down at my borrowed shoes. "You going to take off those monstrosities?"

"These cost hundreds of dollars, I'll have you know."

"Doesn't stop them from looking very uncomfortable." His hand darts out to touch my left ankle.

I'm so surprised, I almost fall over. Again. "What are you doing?"

"Figured you didn't want to sit in the sand and get your dress dirty." His thumb rubs light circles just above my ankle bone and sheesh, why does that tiny flicker flood my whole body with warmth? "Just lean on me and I'll help you."

I don't respond except to do as he suggests, placing my hand on his shoulder as I extend my foot. When he slides off the heel, he doesn't let go of my foot immediately. Instead, his index finger slides down the length of my arch, right where the glass cut me last week. "It's healed up nicely."

He says it so calmly. Meanwhile, I'm shivering from his touch. It's all I can do to stay standing. "Mmm hmm," is my insipid reply.

After he removes my second shoe, he stands and hands both to me. We walk them to the Shoe Check and then turn toward the party. Time to face the happy couple.

My insides start shaking and my shoulders round off. I crumple in on myself as I place my folded hands to my nose and forehead. "I don't think I can do this."

"Hey." Connor curls his fingers around my forearms, gently prying them apart. Then he tilts my chin upward. "Remember, you're the amazing Evie Denmark. You've got a killer job, an awesome support system, and best of all"—he winks—"a sexy boyfriend who loves you."

My gaze darts away from his despite Kayla's warning in my head that I "must maintain eye contact." Because what Connor is saying isn't true. Not the last bit, anyway.

Even though, with each passing interaction, I kind of want it to be.

Ack. What am I doing? Why do I have to keep reminding myself that this is a deal Connor and I struck, nothing more? He's using me to get his manuscript edited and I'm using him to … well, my reasons don't really make sense anymore. Because was it ever *really* about making David jealous or getting Stephanie to feel guilty?

Or was I lying to myself? Was it really about having the opportunity to get close to Connor, a guy I've always secretly admired even though he's never thought of me like *that*?

And of course, it's at that moment when David looks in our direction. His gaze skims right over us, but then his neck snaps back toward me. Rubbing his jaw, he stares for a long few moments, blinking and ignoring the older couple talking to him.

Dressed in a gray suit with no tie, he's still as handsome as ever, though he's gained a tiny bit of padding around his waist and his brown hairline has begun to recede just a tad. Today he's wearing his contacts, and even from afar I can see his blue eyes—the ones I used to love making plenty of eye contact with, the ones I had memorized, the ones I was sure I'd see on my babies one day.

My insides prickle and I bite my lip as we stare at each other.

Then an elegant blonde woman in a white sheath dress walks up and touches his arm—and he doesn't move. Stephanie's doe-like green eyes widen when she turns and sees me. She darts a glance between David and me again before putting on a tight smile and tugging David across the beach toward us.

I want to run far, far away.

But before I can act on the pure adrenaline flooding my system, a hand slides around me, fingers pressing into my waist. Startled, I glance up to find Connor there, tall, solid. He uses his other hand to smooth a flyaway hair out of my eyes. "It's going to be okay."

Then he leans down and kisses me.

His mouth is soft and gentle—and gone before I can process what just happened. I just stand there, literally seeing spots.

Connor Bryant kissed me.

Holy buckets, I want more than just a quick peck. And the grin Connor is wearing tells me he knows his effect on me. He lowers his head once more and I eagerly close my eyes, waiting for another kiss. Instead, Connor whispers, "Let the show begin."

Huh?

A throat clears and my eyes pop open as I spin to face Stephanie and David, who is glaring at Connor.

Oh. The show. Right.

Because this. is. not. real.

Get a grip, Evie. Remember why you're here—even if you don't fully understand it. But whatever my reasons for coming, I'm here. I can sort out my feelings later.

"David, Steph. H-hey."

One of Connor's arms is still around me but he reaches out with his other toward David. "Connor Bryant. Evie's boyfriend." The words wrap their delicious tendrils around me. "Congrats on the upcoming nuptials."

David takes Connor's hand and I can tell he's squeezing hard by the veins popping on his neck. "David Atkinson."

Stephanie looks between the guys, a look of expectation on her face. Then, all too chipper, she injects, "And I'm Stephanie, his fiancée." Turning to me, she tugs me into a hug. "Good to see you, Evie." The woman who once upon a time was my friend pulls back, brows in a downward V. "We weren't sure you would make it."

"Oh, well—"

"I mean, I wouldn't have been surprised." Stephanie shrugs and threads her arm through David's as she leans into him. He's still kind of oblivious—and staring at me. "We know what a workaholic you are. Not that we'd ever ask you to skip work to come to our little shower." She lowers her voice. "We know you need the money to send home to your poor folks."

I'm not sure she understands what it means to have a salaried job—or any real job, for that matter—considering she "works" for her daddy's accounting firm as a receptionist sometimes, when she feels like going in. Still, her words hit their intended target. I find my fingers sliding along the rough edges of my necklace. "I wouldn't have missed it for the world." My false laugh sounds like someone's strangling me.

"Evie, you look …" David tugs at the collar of his shirt and clears his throat. "Different."

He totally misses the evil glare that Steph tosses his way. She puts on a pout and inclines her head back toward me. "Yes, it's really sweet that you got so dressed up for our casual little shindig."

Not even David misses her patronizing tone, if his raised eyebrows are any indication. Just then a waiter walks by carrying a platter full of half-filled red wine glasses and I can't move quickly enough to grab one. Maybe some alcohol will help this night go faster.

Connor, David, and Stephanie all take glasses too.

"So, Connor, what do you do?" Stephanie bats her eyelashes at Connor, and the memory of her doing the same thing to David—*while* we were dating—rises to the surface of my mind.

My whole body tenses and I stare into the abyss of my wine. The cold glass presses against my fingertips as I swirl the liquid inside. With a single swig, I chug it down. The bitter grapes hit my tongue and make me shiver because, oh yeah, I'm super picky about wine and this is way too strong for my liking. But that doesn't stop me from trading my glass with Connor's. Ignoring his surprised laugh, I drink half of his too.

"Um, I'm the marketing director at Evermore."

"Oh, so you know Evie from work?" Stephanie leans in. "Makes sense that's where you met. It's the only place Evie spends her time. We have to practically drag her to dinner to see us, and I can only talk her into it once every six months or so."

My nerves begin to hum. I'm such a lightweight and I haven't eaten much of anything today, so I quickly recognize the heady feeling of an alcohol buzz. But it's warm and it's keeping me from lashing out at Stephanie, so I take another sip while Connor, David, and Stephanie continue this inane conversation.

And another sip, and another, till this glass is drained too.

Someone somewhere calls to David and he turns, waving. "Steph, we'd better go say hi to some of our other guests."

"Right." Steph stares adoringly into David's eyes, and I'm suddenly struck with the urge to cry. Because I can see it so clearly now. She always loved him, was probably only friends with me in order to get close to him. And then, when his interest in me waned—when I'd worked too much and didn't give him enough attention, when he grew tired of my dull looks and quirky personality—of course he'd turned to my vibrant, beautiful friend for companionship.

How did I *ever* consider her a friend?

She's just another example of what a terrible judge of character I am.

But before the tears threatening to fall can hit my cheek, I remember Kayla's words. *"If you start feeling depressed, you power pose the crap out of tonight."*

And that's why, like a crazy person, I widen my stance and lift my arms in a V like I'm celebrating a victory.

But here's the thing about being buzzed-slash-drunk. It's possible that you forget that you're holding things—for instance, a wine glass. It's also possible that said wine glass isn't as empty as you'd thought.

An arc of unfinished alcohol arcs through the air right toward Stephanie's white dress.

Sploosh.

Stumbling backward, Stephanie looks down at the splatters of red on her outfit and curses. Beside me, Connor is holding back a laugh. David is standing there, eyebrows lifted.

And I've got my hand over my mouth, my eyes wide with horror. "I'm so sorry. I didn't mean to do that. Really."

Her nostrils flare but somehow she holds in her anger—words wise, at least. Her murderous eyes are another story. "Of course, you didn't. If you'll excuse me, I need to see if I can get this out before it sets."

She turns on her heel and stalks toward the country club building, David following on her heels like a puppy dog.

Then Connor breaks down, his guffaw slightly muffled as he tugs me into a hug and laughs into my hair. "That was brilliant."

And where moments ago I'd been tempted to bawl, now I grow very tired and comfortable as I snuggle against him. If I were a cat, I'd be purring. My hands, which are pressed against his chest, drift under his jacket and glide across his silky shirt until they find their way around his taut waist. As I breathe in his rich cologne, my fingers inch up his back, skimming his shoulders all the way from the top of his spine to his amazingly defined deltoid muscles.

Connor's body goes stock-still and I feel his heart-beat increase. We stand like that for several minutes, the rest of the party noise swirling around us. It's just the two of us, under the stars, and I have no idea what is going on.

But I am here for it.

Finally, I speak the words that float to the top of my heart. "Thank you. I …" But I can't manage the rest. Not without breaking the spell. Not without crying.

He shifts, pulling back slightly so he can look at me. His eyes study me for one second, two, but then he blinks and steps away, massaging the back of his neck. "Of course. Just fulfilling my end of the deal."

The warmth of the moment is splashed with cold water, and my whole body is suddenly heavy. I place a hand on my belly. "Can you please take me home now? I don't feel so good."

And the cause isn't merely the sloshing wine on an empty stomach—but Connor doesn't need to know that.

eight

. . .

ALL WEEK, I've managed to keep things professional between Connor and me.

Of course, it helps that I'm still working from home and have kept uber busy helping Justine finish up an edit.

Still, today I plan to maintain that professionalism. There is absolutely no reason to be awkward around him. So what that we kissed (Kayla later that night: "I demand to know why there was no tongue action!") and I became embarrassingly clingy (I blame the booze!)? That's all water under the bridge.

You think if I say a thing enough times, it becomes true? (Asking for a friend.)

Regardless, today I step out of Kayla's Prius (I'm still waiting for insurance to pay for a replacement car since mine was totaled in the landslide) and walk toward the Japanese Friendship Garden in Balboa Park. Apparently Connor processes better when moving, so he's invited me to take a stroll before diving into my manuscript critiques.

When I told my housemates, they waggled their eyebrows and called it a date.

I'm certain it's NOT.

Because wouldn't a guy who was interested in me send more than one text the last seven days? Wouldn't he have kissed me senseless when he dropped me off after the wedding shower a week ago?

Exactly. The serial-dater-slash-huge-flirt didn't give me a second thought. Or maybe he's just smarter than me.

Because liking someone you work with is a bad, bad idea—especially when you're up for the same promotion.

As I walk down the street toward the garden, I puff out my chest and hold my arms in the air. Yeah, Kayla's power poses got me into trouble at the shower, but they do give me a surprising burst of confidence after a while. By the time I see Connor standing near the entrance to the garden and drop my arms back to my sides, I feel powerful. We're about to talk story, and that's my area of expertise. I know this stuff. I can help him improve his book.

I've got this.

And afterward, I'll have fulfilled my end of the bargain. Our deal will be half over and I won't be beholden to him anymore.

He waves and darn it if he doesn't look as good in chino shorts, a navy T-shirt that hugs his muscles, and a pair of boat shoes as he does in a suit. At least today I'm all covered up, although I did allow Kayla to pick out my white shorts, pink smocked waist top with flutter sleeves, and jeweled sandals. I feel pretty and girly, and Connor's appreciative look as I come closer gives me an extra boost. "Hi."

"Hey, there." For a second, it looks like he might go in for a hug, but then changes his mind. "Thanks for meeting here. This place always calms me, so I thought it would be a good place to meet while you rip my story to shreds."

I laugh, thankful that things are more relaxed between us than the last time we saw each other. "I don't rip stories to shreds."

"Sure, you don't." He winks and turns. "Come on. I already bought our tickets."

I follow him past the Tea Pavilion restaurant and through the front entrance, where we begin to stroll the path. Thankfully, because we came early, the garden isn't all that crowded yet, and the hum of quiet is just what I need for the stress of the workweek to melt away. As we explore the luscious garden, the small gravel crunches beneath our feet and water trickles down rock-strewn streams.

I gasp as a grouping of cherry blossom trees in full bloom comes into view. The air is filled with the perfume of their scent, and I stop, close my eyes, and breathe it in. When I finally open them again, I feel Connor's gaze on me. I turn to find him unabashedly staring at me, but then he breaks our eye contact. "Pretty nice, huh?"

"I think it's … pulchritudinous." I smirk.

He leans closer and drops his voice to a husky undertone. "You're pulchritudinous, Webster."

My stomach drops to my feet. *Keep it professional, remember, Evie?*

"What's that mean, anyway?" He winks and starts walking down the path again.

I'm seriously so confused. Does he know *pulchritudinous* means beautiful or is he just messing with me? Neither? Both? My head hurts as I rush to keep up with him. We walk under an arch of sweetly scented purple wisteria hanging in clusters over our heads.

Connor reaches up and touches one. "This was my mom's favorite flower."

"It's beautiful."

"Some might even call it *pulchritudinous*." A sad smile inks its way across his lips, and in that moment, two things are confirmed.

One: There is so much more to Connor Bryant than I ever thought possible.

And two: I want to know it. All of it.

But can I trust myself? I clearly don't have the best track record with men—or people in general. I trust too easily. Give my heart too quickly.

And in the past, it's cost me in big ways.

But right now, I don't much care about all of that, which is why I lay my hand on Connor's arm. "You said it *was* your mom's favorite. Did she …" I lick my lips. "Is she …?"

"Yeah." Connor stares down at my hand for a few seconds before reaching for it. He keeps hold of it as we stand looking up at the wisteria. "Ten years ago. Just before I moved to San Diego to take the job at Evermore. Breast cancer."

"I'm so sorry." I squeeze his hand.

He weaves our fingers together, his gaze still on the flowers. "She was the only reason I moved back to Los Angeles after graduating college. Once she was gone, I had no reason to be there anymore."

"Is your dad gone too?"

"No." His lips go flat and he huffs. "And my older brother lives in New York. He's a family man and a surgeon—someone my dad can really be proud of."

"I'm sure he's proud of you too."

He finally finds my gaze again, an amused but pained smile on his lips. "You're sure, huh?" Then Connor cocks his head. "You think the best of everyone, don't you?"

And it's been my downfall. "Well." My voice squeaks. I desperately need to change the subject. "I haven't always thought the best of you." Then I do an outrageous thing—I wink.

The tension breaks and he lets loose a relieved laugh. "I haven't always given you a reason to, have I?" Then he starts walking again and I'm right there with him, still hand in hand, wondering where in the world we are going—where *this* is going.

"Trust yourself." Kayla's voice is in my head again. We did more "confidence lessons" this week and her words keep popping randomly into my brain at the most inopportune times.

But this time, I choose to listen. To relax. To just … be.

After we've walked most of the garden, Connor tugs me toward a bench in front of a koi pond. He places his arm along the back of the seat and turns his body toward me, finally letting go of my hand. "So, time to lay it on me. How bad is my book?"

The sun is higher in the sky now, its rays breaking across the garden and adding a sparkle to the pond. "It's not bad at all. Actually, I loved it. Well." I place my hands on my knees. "Except for one thing. Okay, two."

"And what are those?" He crosses his leg with his top foot pointed toward me. According to Kayla's body language exercises, that means he wants to be closer. If he didn't, he'd have crossed his legs the opposite way.

Stop reading into every little thing and just enjoy the moment.

Right.

"Okay, well the first is more of a question. I know it's a personal choice, but why not use your real name? Why a pen name?"

He huffs. "My dad."

"Your dad? I don't get it."

"What's the second thing?"

Okay. Touchy subject, obviously. Hopefully he won't take offense to my next critique. "The ending."

His shoe—the one that is now hovering close to my knee—taps my hands. "You didn't like it?"

"Did I like when the main character left the woman he loved behind because he wanted the best for her? No. I hated it and so will every romance reader who picks up your book."

Connor raises his eyebrows. "I thought it was poignant. Sacrificial. Noble."

"Forget that." Waving my hand in the air, I scoot closer to him—not realizing I've done it until it's too late. But I have to make him understand this point or his career as a romance author is over before it's begun. "Romance readers want an HEA."

"A what?"

"An HEA. Happily ever after."

"But that's not realistic."

Oh no. Is he one of *those*—a romance author who doesn't believe in love? "I don't agree with you, but let's just say for a minute that what you said is true. Here's the thing—it doesn't matter. Romance readers read to escape. They don't want realistic. They want adorable and romantic and passionate and all the feels."

"You're really getting fired up there, Webster."

"Clearly I feel strongly about the subject." I smile. "But I'm serious. The hero needs to sacrifice for the heroine in such a way that they can be together in the end."

His nose scrunches. "But what if he's just not good enough for her?"

"He needs to be or we won't love him in the first place." I can't help it—I grab his crossed foot and shake it. "Connor, your hero *is* good enough. No, he's not perfect, but he is perfect for the heroine. And he's a good man. He just doesn't see it for himself. That's why he needs her."

"Because she makes him a better man?"

"Yes and no." I consider my words. "I think rather

than her changing him, she goes on a journey with him toward that change. She's the encourager, the cheerleader, the truth teller." Now the words are rolling off my tongue. "She sees things in him that no one else sees, and it's she alone who can help him see that he's been believing a lie all this time. Because when she looks at him, she doesn't see a failure. She sees a man who is worthy of love—a man who is good simply because he is himself."

"Evie." And then he's looking at me with such longing that I feel it all the way down to my toes. "Does a woman like that really exist?" He shakes his head. "I mean, of course she does. My mom was like that, even though I never thought my dad deserved her love. But I guess I wonder ..." He's quiet, contemplating something much deeper.

Much more personal, if I had to hazard a guess.

I swallow. "What is it you wonder?"

But he's far away, and either doesn't hear me or doesn't want to answer. So we sit there in companionable silence for a while, watching the fish swimming in the koi pond. The garden is getting more crowded now and our peaceful retreat is broken.

Connor stands. "You ready to go?"

I'm disappointed that we didn't get to delve deeper, but he's clearly not ready. Maybe he never will be. "Sure." I follow him back down the winding path and out through the gate as we return to the parking lot.

When we come to his car first, he looks around. "Where are you parked?"

I point across the lot. "Over there."

Connor pulls his keys from his pocket and flips them around in his palm. "Hop in. I'll give you a ride."

"It's not that far."

"Come on, Webster. Just let me give you a ride." Then he unlocks the doors and ducks inside.

And because I don't want our time together to end, I follow suit. The inside of his car smells like him—warm and citrusy—and I buckle myself in.

But he doesn't put the key in the ignition. Instead, he turns toward me, his hand on the wheel. "Can you send me your notes on the book?"

"Of course." I tap the seatbelt buckle with my fingernail as I wait for him to drive.

But still he sits there, considering me. In here, we're closed off from the world, and it's a cocoon from everything that might distract us.

It suddenly feels very intimate. And his gaze, it's intense, slowly burning fire through my veins until I have to look away.

"Evie."

"Yeah?" I study the gray car dash as if it's the most fascinating thing in the world.

"You're pretty great, you know that?"

His words unleash a thousand butterflies in my stomach. I run a sweaty palm down my leg. *He means you're a great editor. That's it.* "Um, thank you."

"Which is why I don't understand why you allow your ex and his fiancée to treat you like garbage."

Huh? My eyes dart back to him. Where had that thought come from? "I thought we were talking about your story."

"We are. Kind of." He frowns. "Has no one ever told you that *you're* good enough—that you don't need to put up with idiotic jerks and the trash they spew?"

The muscles in my stomach are acting like they're at the track and field Olympics and it's time to jump hurdles.

"I mean it. Don't you know that you're twice the woman that Stephanie is?"

My heart is seriously about to beat out of my chest, and I'm sure I resemble a trout the way my mouth is flopping open. I've never heard Connor Bryant talk to a woman like this. Flirt and falsely compliment? Sure. But this is … deeper.

And I think he feels it too, because suddenly he's clenching his jaw and making a fist that taps the steering wheel. "I loved a girl like Stephanie once. Beautiful, effervescent—how's that one for you, Webster?—and cruel."

There's pain in his eyes as he tells his story. I settle my cheek against my seat's headrest and watch him, longing to reach out and smooth away the frown lines framing his eyes. "What happened?"

"We were high school sweethearts. Together for three years. I was supposed to play basketball at USC. Had a scholarship and everything. But Victoria, she was going to Florida State, and she begged me to come with her." His fingers rub his stubbled neck, right over his Adam's apple. "I was head over heels and afraid to lose her, so I decided to follow Victoria to the Sunshine State."

I have a bad feeling about where this is going.

"She broke up with me after two months on campus. Two months. Apparently she liked all the shiny new objects that Florida had to offer." He shakes his head. "And I was the dummy with a broken heart, now stuck paying out-of-state tuition at a school that didn't hold any interest for me. I transferred to another school after the first year and made myself a promise."

"What promise?" I feel like I'm reading a novel and at the very crucial moment when we find out the hero's wound—the thing that has kept him from being able to love the heroine.

"To never again give up anything I want for anyone else—especially a woman."

Boom. Mic drop.

But instead of feeling happy that I finally understand Connor a bit more, a rock settles in my stomach. "Why are you telling me all of this?"

He runs a hand through his hair. "I don't know. Just … don't let people take advantage of you or treat you like you're nothing." His eyes trace my face and the urgency in his expression steals my breath. "Don't let them diminish your glow, because you'd be robbing this world of a lot of light if you do."

Kill me now. I can die happy.

And I can't deny it anymore—don't want to deny it.

Connor Bryant is the unexpected hero in this story, the one unfolding before my eyes.

He just doesn't know it yet.

nine

· · ·

IT'S BEEN eighteen days since I admitted to myself that I am falling in love with Connor Bryant.

But who's counting, right?

I haven't seen him since that day in the garden, though we've texted quite a bit—mostly to make plans for attending the wedding in three days (eek!) and also to chat about his manuscript, which he's been furiously working on and improving.

Still, I've analyzed those quiet moments together over and over in my mind. And of course, I recounted them to Kayla, who stood and did a victory dance for being right.

"About what?" I demanded.

"I knew you liked him, but were too stubborn to admit it." She wiggled her hips, her hands raised in a V over her head. *"And I knew he liked yooooooou."*

"I'm not sure that he does." But the idea is thrilling.

"Trust me. A guy doesn't open up like that to just anyone."

"What if … I don't know. What if he's just trying to …" I couldn't even say the words. They were too awful to think.

"What? To sleep with you?" She rolled her eyes. "Please. If all he wanted was sex, there are plenty of females in San Diego who would willingly throw themselves his way. I mean, have you seen the man?" Kayla fanned herself.

Of course at that moment, Lauren joined us and I was forced to tell the whole story again. Lauren joined Kayla in the fanning, adding a proper dramatic fainting hand on her forehead as she plopped back against the couch. "He's dreamy, that's for sure."

"And he likes you, Evie."

"Oh, he totally does," Lauren said. "The way he looked at you when he picked you off the floor before the shower date was just so … well, if a man looked at me like that, I'd tell him right then and there that I wanted to have his babies."

I tucked my arms around my middle. "I don't know." Because I thought David liked me too. Loved me.

And I was dead wrong on that score.

Kayla squeezed my arm. "If you don't trust yourself, trust me."

And even though doubts try to get under my skin, I do trust her.

Which is why my insides are twisted with both excitement and terror as I walk down the hallway of our office building for the first time since the earthquake over a month ago. I head toward Connor's office, clutching my most recent edits of his manuscript. He probably isn't in just yet, but I'll just drop the notes off—

along with a special something I've tied to the top with some twine.

But before I can knock on his door, Lisa calls me from her office. I straighten my blazer and walk through my boss's open doorway. "Hey! Good to see you again."

"Yes, it's good to be back together." But Lisa isn't smiling like it's good. She's smiling like she has bad news to deliver. "Please shut the door and take a seat."

Oh no. Has she decided to give the promotion to Connor? The last month, being out of the office, I kind of lost myself in work and was able to shut out the worry over making more money except for the few times I talked with my parents (and after those phone calls, I stuffed my face full of ice cream and watched BBC shows until my anxiety drifted away—especially because my dad's other hip is hurting now and he really needs to get a replacement but can't afford to take time off work).

But now? We're back to reality, and I can't help but wonder if my dreams are about to die a quick and painful death. After doing as Lisa asked, I hold Connor's manuscript in my lap. "What's up?"

Lisa leans forward, elbows on the desk, looks like she's going to say something but then gets distracted by the orange package attached to the manuscript. "Are you bribing one of our authors with Reese's Pieces?"

My lips quirk as I run my fingertips over the treat I bought to give Connor some extra fuel during his edits. "Something like that." I try to sit taller like Kayla taught me, even spreading my arms out to the side momentarily. "You're making me nervous, Lisa." Might as well rip off the Band-Aid. "Did you already make your decision about the promotion?"

"Not yet."

I release a breath I didn't realize I'd been holding. "Okay." Then what is this about?

It's like she hears the question I don't say aloud because she steeples her fingers and places them over her mouth for a moment. "Evie, you are a wonderful editor. A wonderful person. But I've heard through the grapevine that you've been doing a lot of your editors' work for them."

My jaw drops. Who else even knows that? And who would tattle on me? Surely not Connor.

No. I'm not going to believe it of him. I may not have a great track record with men, maybe have trusted the wrong ones in the past, but Connor is different.

He is *different, right?*

"Um, well, I've jumped in and helped when my team needed me."

"At some point, you're going to have to trust your team to do their own work."

"What?" Is that what she thinks this is about? Sally and Justine, they came to me *asking* for help—I didn't foist it upon them. But I don't want to throw them under the bus. "Of course I trust them. But they were coming up on their deadlines and needed me to jump in." I hold up my hands. "And I didn't mind. I *don't* mind. I'll do anything to make sure Evermore is successful."

"I know you will." Lisa sets her hands back on the desk, her fingers splayed. Can fingers have power poses too? I'll have to ask Kayla. "But I need you to understand that a good leader delegates tasks. She doesn't take them all on herself, because she realizes that she is limited in her time and abilities."

I truly don't know what to say. I thought I was doing a good job, thought I was helping my team. Maybe I've just been enabling them, though. My brow scrunches as I play with the twine in my lap. "How do you know the line between helping and hindering?"

"You're a good person, Evie. I know you want to make everything easier for everyone else around you."

I swallow.

"But sometimes, you can't. Sometimes you have to let others feel the consequences of their own actions." Lisa smiles, but there's something sad in it—like maybe there's more of a story behind the words. "Sometimes you have to admit that you can't solve everyone else's problems. All you can do is be there for them, to support them. And that's what a good manager does. That's what I need to see you doing if you really want this promotion to associate publisher."

"I do." I say it so quickly, I almost believe it.

Because I'll admit that Kayla's question at the coffee shop—which feels like ages ago—about whether I really want the job has stayed lodged in the back of my brain, refusing to leave.

Besides, change is scary. And I don't know if I have what it really takes to be an associate publisher. I don't want to let down my team. Lisa. The company.

And yet, I still feel the same way about the promise I made to my parents. I owe it to them.

"I'm glad to hear it."

As I'm leaving Lisa's office, I catch a light under the door of Connor's office, and the urge to see him overwhelms me. I wish I could tell him all the things I'm feeling, but it would be too much—after all, I don't want to scare him away. Maybe we'll get a chance to talk more deeply this weekend during our date at the wedding. I know I need to stay focused on the promotion, but I'll allow myself this one indulgence—this one thing to look forward to that isn't work—and who knows? More might come out of it. Maybe he'll give me another peek into his soul.

My grip tightens around his manuscript as I approach his office, but just then my cell phone vibrates in my pocket. Who would be calling me this early? Of course my parents are several hours ahead—what if something is wrong? One-handed, I yank out the phone.

Stephanie.

Stephanie? What in the world? I haven't talked to her since spilling wine all over her clothes. "Hello?" I try not to speak too loudly. Some of my co-workers are not early morning people and hate noise before they've consumed their a.m. coffee.

"Oh, thank goodness," Stephanie says. "Evie, you've got to save me."

Huh? Has she finally figured out that David isn't worth marrying?

Whoa. Did I seriously just think that? Huh. Maybe Connor's words about my ex have actually sunk in. "What's going on, Steph? Are you okay?"

"No, I'm not okay. My cousin Marlee was just in a car accident."

"Oh my goodness. Is she all right?" I don't know Marlee. She might be one of Stephanie's East Coast cousins.

"I mean, she's fine, like alive and stuff." Stephanie huffs out a breath. "But she broke both of her legs, which means she can't come to the wedding."

"Okay." And I need to know this because …?

"And that means I'm down a bridesmaid, Evie! David refuses to un-ask one of his groomsmen to stand up with him, and I can't have uneven numbers—which means I need a new bridesmaid, stat!"

My knees threaten to collapse. "And …" *Please don't say it, please don't say it.*

"You and Marlee are the same size! And there's no one else I know who wouldn't need the dress majorly taken in and there just isn't time for that considering the wedding is only days away. Please, please, would you fill in?"

I try to ignore the sting in her words. Sure, I'm not a size zero like she is, but I'm not exactly obese. And even if I were, she doesn't have the right to treat me like this. Connor's words from the garden drift back to me: *"Don't let people take advantage of you or treat you like you're nothing."*

I open my mouth to say I can't do it, but she plows on just like Steam Engine Stephanie always does. "And before you say no, I just want to … well, Evie, I know I should have said this before, but I'm sorry. I'm so sorry that I put David above our friendship. So sorry that we hurt you with this relationship. I hope you know that was never the intention."

Slumping against the office wall, I grit my teeth and close my eyes against the tears burning behind my lids. How long have I wanted my old friend to acknowledge that? I've ached for this apology more than I let myself admit. "I … thanks, Stephanie."

"I don't want you to think I'm saying it just because I need you." She sighs. "I miss you. And I should have said I'm sorry a long time ago."

"I miss you too." Sure, we were never as close as Kayla and me, but some of my best memories of California are of me, David, and Stephanie hanging out together. "As for being your bridesmaid …" I still don't quite know what to say on that front. Being part of the wedding party sounds fairly miserable, honestly, and I was so looking forward to spending that time with Connor.

And if I'm a bridesmaid, I'd feel weird about asking him to come since I'd be so busy. Plus, now that Stephanie and I have sort-of-kind-of "made up," I'm not sure I need Connor to come along—but I don't want to have to tell him that either.

Ugh. My head hurts. "Can I have the morning to think about it?"

"Sure, yeah, of course." Stephanie pauses, her voice softening. "I never would have asked if you hadn't moved on. But seeing you with Connor the other night … well, David and I are both really happy for you."

Oh man, I can't keep the tears in any longer. Not only because I don't know if what Connor and I have is real—or could be real—but because finally being at peace with Stephanie and David feels like a gift I didn't think I'd ever receive. "Thanks, Steph. I'm happy for you too."

We hang up and I wipe my tears away. I need to talk with Connor about the wedding, see what he thinks. I actually really care about his opinion now. Probably dumb of me, but I kind of think the bond we've formed over the last month means he cares about mine too.

I step toward his office, which is cracked open, stick my head inside—and freeze.

Connor is in his chair and the receptionist, June, is sitting on his desk right beside him. Despite her back facing me, I can see that she's wearing a skirt that rides halfway up her thigh and giggling as she twirls her hair.

Neither of them notices me, and it's no wonder—Connor is staring so intently into June's eyes that I think he might kiss her.

My stomach is on a rollercoaster and right now, it's at the hanging-upside-down-hold-on-for-dear-life part. I should leave—I want to leave—but my legs won't move.

"June, do you know what *pulchritudinous* means?"

I want to throw up right now. He's using *my* word to flirt with another woman.

He's the same old guy. Why did I think he might change just because we hung out a few times?

She giggles again and swings her shapely legs. "Polka-what?"

Move, you stupid feet. Move! Finally, my body listens, but as I back out, my elbow hits the door frame and I gasp with the pain of hitting my funny bone—which is *so* not a funny thing to hit, by the way.

Connor and June turn toward me, and Connor's eyes widen. "Evie. Hey." He looks at the package in my hands and his gaze seems to soften, but I don't trust myself to read him right. "Is that for me?"

"Yes." Somehow I find the strength to move forward and place the manuscript and Reese's Pieces on his desk. "I've got those changes for you."

June tries to peek at the manuscript, but Connor turns it over. He keeps his gaze on me. "Thank you. I look forward to chatting with you about this. And thanks for the Reese's. You remembered."

I seriously want to take that package of candy and chuck it at his head. He has no business looking at me like I'm special when he was just in here calling June beautiful—and doing who knows what else. "No problem. Just fulfilling my end of the bargain."

"What bargain?" June leans toward Connor and touches his shoulder, her lips in a pout.

But he basically ignores her, his eyes and mouth frowning at me. "Are you okay, Webster?"

Am I okay? Seriously?

Argh, this man!

And in that moment, I know what I need to do. I need to let him go. I need to focus on the promotion like I should have been doing all this time.

I need to end our bargain before it ends me.

"I'm fine. I just got a call from Stephanie and she needs a fill-in bridesmaid." I notch up my chin, pretending to be brave. Fake it till you make it, right? "So I won't be needing an escort anymore."

"What?" Connor stands and June nearly tumbles off the desk. Her head is bouncing between us like there's an invisible ping-pong ball flying through the air.

"I'm going to—"

"I heard you." He rounds the desk, like a lion stalking his prey. I take a step backward. "I just can't believe you're letting her take advantage of you like that. She snaps and you come running like a little puppy dog."

"That's not true." And I can feel my eyes flashing. I don't like conflict, but right now he's cornering me—and if I'm some sort of puppy dog, I'm about to bare my teeth and attack. "She apologized for everything."

"And you just forgave her?"

"Some of us understand the meaning of the word." And as I say it, I know I've gone too far. Because whatever is going on between Connor and his dad … well, maybe it's not as forgivable as what Stephanie did to me. I have no right to judge him for holding onto his hurt. "Oh, Connor, I'm sorry. I didn't mean it."

"I think you did." By now, my back is against the wall, and he leans in with his voice lowered. "And you know what? I'm proud of you. You're finally standing up for yourself. With me, anyway. I just wish you'd do the same with other people. It's okay to say no. It's okay to go after what you want."

But how can I go after what I want when what I want doesn't want me back?

I'm nearly weak with the closeness of him, the way

he's not even touching me and I'm still on fire. How can I be so upset with him one minute, and wanting to kiss him the next?

I'm such a mess.

And I've got to get out of here, because Connor makes me forget myself. Makes me lose focus.

I duck and run from his office as quickly as I can. Then I make a phone call. "Steph? I'm in."

ten

REMIND me to never be a bridesmaid again.

At the ripe age of thirty-two, I don't know how I've managed to avoid the duty thus far, but as I sit here a few hours into the reception, fanning myself with a discarded dinner menu—my bare feet propped up on an empty chair—I can honestly say I'm grateful that none of my closest friends has ever gotten married yet.

Or maybe it's just that Stephanie has kind of been a Bridezilla.

Not only did she ask us to stay super late after the rehearsal dinner last night finishing up wedding favors, but all eight of the bridesmaids (yes, eight!) had to be at her beachside hotel room at seven a.m. sharp this morning. We also each had to bring a brunch item to share. My offering of donuts was not looked upon kindly by the matchstick women serving as the other bridesmaids (so I ate three ... shhh, don't tell!).

Then, we had hair and makeup done by professionals, photos, gifts, and a thousand other little errands that I can't recall now as a host of drunk people do the Macarena on the dance floor and I hide out at an empty table next to another occupied by Stephanie's relatives who are too old to dance.

The hotel ballroom is exceptionally gorgeous, with an entire wall of windows facing the ocean and a balcony overlooking the beach below. Decor-wise, the coral and white accents are divine—I really can't imagine a more beautiful wedding. Somehow, I made it through the ceremony and dinner without feeling too sorry for myself. I just tried to focus on being the bigger person, even when Stephanie snapped at me for not knowing how to properly tie up her bustle. (She promptly apologized and blamed it on the stress of her big day, so all is well now.)

And I've tried very hard not to miss Connor tonight. During a lull in visitors to the head table, Stephanie asked me where he was and I simply said he couldn't make it after all. Of course, after our "chat" on Wednesday, he tried several times to talk to me about the wedding, but I went home early and then took off Thursday and yesterday to help with wedding stuff. I know he just felt bad he couldn't hold up his end of the bargain, especially since I've spent so much time this last month critiquing his manuscript. But it was my call.

My heart on the line.

Not that he knows that.

I sigh and take another sip of champagne, one arm crossed over the other as I observe happy couples on the dance floor shift into a slow dance. They sway to Sinatra's "The Way You Look Tonight" and I have never felt so on the outside of things—so on the outskirts of love.

Closing my eyes, I let the melody wash over me. And then, someone touches my elbow. I glance up and nearly spill my drink at the sight of Connor standing there in a suit I've never seen before—and goodness, he looks even better than the wedding cake I devoured minutes ago.

And I want a piece of *that*.

"Connor?" Did I somehow summon him from the wishful depths of my heart?

He squats next to me. "Hey, Webster." But no, that sultry voice is very real. "You're a hard woman to track down."

"What do you mean?"

Chuckling, he shakes his head. "You only told me the venue was at 'a beachside hotel.' I've spent the last few days calling around, trying to find the right one. And when that didn't work, I finally got so desperate that I showed up at your house and begged Kayla to tell me. Sorry I'm late, but traffic getting up here was a beast."

I'm still processing what he's told me. "You went to my house?" Licking my lips, I place the champagne flute on the table. "Why would you do that?"

He snags a full champagne glass next to me and takes a swig. "A deal's a deal, Webster."

Oh.

"I released you from that deal."

"Maybe I don't want to be released from it."

Oh!

He holds out his hand and stands. "Dance with me?"

I study him for a moment. I mean, he looks sincere. But that doesn't mean he *wants* to dance with me. Maybe he's just feeling guilty for all the time I spent working on his book, and wants to repay me somehow.

But I guess he *is* here. And it would be nice to dance.

Without answering, I let him help me out of this chair. But before I can slip my heels back on, he shakes his head. "I like you barefoot." His gaze roams my whole body, taking in the A-line coral chiffon dress I'm wearing. Despite the deep-V back and slit up in front, I actually feel really comfortable in it—almost like a princess. It's fun and flirty and pools at my feet, and I love the beaded detailing on the waistline.

Adele's version of "Make You Feel My Love" starts to play as we approach the crowded dance floor. Connor's hands slide around my waist and he gathers me close as I place my hands around his neck.

Then we move. And you know when a couple dances in a movie—and it's like there's no one else in the room?

Yup.

Same right now.

I forget where I am. I forget who is around us. I forget that I'm at the wedding of my ex and the friend who stole him from me.

All I know is Connor. The way he smells like some sort of cologne ad model. The way his fingers are warm against my sides and back. The way the prickly hairs at the base of his neck feel beneath my fingers because I can't help but touch them.

The way Connor softly sings the words of the song for only me to hear. His lips graze my ear and I'm basically a puddle on the dance floor.

I'd let you hold me for a million years, Connor, if it feels like this.

His singing stops during the instrumental bridge, and he shifts his head slightly so that his cheek is pressed against mine. And with every second that passes, he seems to turn his neck a tiny fraction of an inch, so that eventually his lips are resting right next to the little dip at the corner of my mouth.

Before I can think of the consequences, I move the final fraction of an inch so our lips meet full on.

For a moment, he doesn't react—I must have stunned him. But then his hand leaves my waist and cups my face, and his lips are moving with mine in a dance all their own. It's sweet and it's lovely and it's everything that a first real kiss should be.

If it's actually real.

But maybe for him, it's once again for show. Because he agreed to be here with me as my "boyfriend."

I break away from him, out of his arms. We look at each other, silent, and I realize the song has ended. The DJ is saying something about a wedding game they're going to play with the bride and groom.

"Want some fresh air?" Connor asks.

I nod, unable to speak, my lips swollen.

He leads me out to the balcony, where a few other people linger in the darkening shadows. The ocean brushes in and out, a constant motion that calms my racing heart. We move to the edge of the balcony, facing the beach, and lean against the balustrade shoulder to shoulder. Wind teases my hair around my face.

What do I say now? No idea. So I say nothing, allowing the wash of the ocean below to skim the coast, its sound filling the night air around us.

"Hey, Evie?"

I glance at him, but he's still watching the water. "Yeah?"

"Thanks for agreeing to this deal. I know you didn't have to, but …" He swallows, the profile of his Grecian nose strong against the inky night sky. "I'm really glad I've gotten to know you better. And I've been so grateful for your help with my manuscript."

The manuscript. A safe topic. My shoulders relax. "Are you about ready to submit?" It had been nearly ready when I'd dropped it off Wednesday. But I don't want to think about that day. I want to think about this one, right here, right now, where we're the only two people in our world.

He nods, peeks at me, his eyes bright in the starlight. "I couldn't have done it without you."

"Sure you could have. But I'm glad you didn't."

"And I've decided to use my real name. Not a pen name."

"Yeah?"

"Yeah." His brow furrows. "It won't make my dad happy, but that's okay. I'm done trying to please him." He laughs. "Well, I say that, and yet it's probably ninety percent of the reason why I want the associate publisher promotion—to show him that I can succeed outside of his plan for me."

He hasn't mentioned his dad since our time at the garden. "What's the story there?"

"Nah, I don't want to ruin this night by talking about him."

His sad smile prompts me to grab his hand. "Okay."

"But ..." Connor studies me, and his free hand grabs a strand of my hair. He filters it between his index finger and thumb. "What about you? Why do you want the position? Because from what I can tell, you wouldn't get to do much editing—and that seems to be your passion."

We haven't talked much about the fact we're going after the same job, but right now, I don't feel the competition. Because he's just a boy asking to see my heart—and I want to show him. Even if it's painful.

I grip his hand as my lips tremble. "You know how my parents own a dairy farm?"

He nods.

"They're stretched pretty thin and getting older. Dad's had some health issues. Nothing overly serious, but they exist. They've had some financial setbacks too that come with relying on Mother Nature and the always-changing economy for their income—cow diseases, fluctuating dairy prices, that kind of thing. And I need to make more money than I do now so I can hire someone to help them out. Either that, or go home and do it myself."

"You'd give up being an editor?"

"If I have to." My voice trembles and I look briefly toward the horizon.

"Why does it have to fall on your shoulders?"

"I love them. It's my duty as a daughter—the only daughter they have left." I hesitate, breathe in a shudder. "And because I'm the reason my sister is dead."

He lifts my hand to his lips and kisses my knuckles, ever so gently, ever so patiently. "I highly doubt that. You couldn't hurt a fly."

A tear falls down my cheek and I push it away. "Not on purpose, no. But I trust too easily. I've been like that my whole life, you know? And sometimes it comes back to bite me. Or hurt those I love." More tears fall and Connor's thumb pushes them away.

"What happened?"

And I allow myself to go back there, to that night when I failed my sister—my whole family. "I was thirteen. My sister was seventeen, and I wanted to be just like her. She was confident, cool, and popular. Basically, my total opposite." I try for a wry grin, but it feels wrong. "One night, I caught her sneaking out with this guy my parents had forbidden her to see. I ran outside to his car, told them they couldn't go. But he turned to me and … I don't know how to explain it except he complimented me and charmed me. And I couldn't tell …" My voice wavers again. "I didn't know he was drunk."

"Oh, Evie." Connor gathers me fully in his arms then. "Car accident?"

I nod and we stand there for who knows how long as the ocean does its thing—being constant, being calm, being peace itself. "So now you know why I can't let my parents lose their farm. They've already lost enough because of me. And if there's a way for me to prevent them from losing anything else, I will."

"I understand how you'd feel that way, but you were just a kid." His palms rub circles into my back. "You can't blame yourself for that. Blame the idiot who drove drunk."

"If I'd just run back inside, told my parents, they could have tracked them down before the accident. They saw him for what he was. Why didn't I?"

"Because you, Evie Denmark, are an amazing human who sees the best in everyone." Connor inhales a sharp breath and tightens his grip on me. "Even me."

"That's because there's a lot of good to see."

"I wish that were true. But you, Webster … you make me want to try."

And I can't help asking, because I have to know if I'm the only woman he's saying this to. "Does June also make you want to try?" Ugh. I hate how small my voice sounds in this moment.

He pulls back, looks into my eyes, confusion clear on his face. "Why would you ask me that?"

I feel stupid but I need to clarify. It'll eat me alive if I don't. "The other day, in your office. You called her pulchritudinous."

And then he's grinning. "Why, Evie Denmark. I do believe you're jealous."

First of all, he sounds like some sort of southern gentleman—a hot one. Second of all, of course I'm jealous! But I don't want to let him know that. I back away, out of his arms. "I just want to know your intentions."

Oh my gosh, I didn't just say that. What am I, a

Regency-era debutante? "You know what? Never mind." I turn to head back inside, the beautiful moment between us broken.

But he snags my elbow and spins me toward him, making my dress flare outward in a twirl. "I didn't call June pulchritudinous. I asked if she knew what it meant. And I could tell by the look on her face that she didn't."

"Okay …" I still don't understand.

"But *you* know what it means, Evie."

Huh?

Now he's chuckling and holding my upper arms. "I don't know any other woman like you, and I love that you're unique."

All right, then.

"And as for my intentions"—he gives a little tug until I'm in his arms again—"I don't really know where this is going, but I'd like the chance to find out. To get to know you." He pauses. "Have dinner with me sometime?"

"Yes." It's all I can manage.

"Next Saturday?"

"Yes."

Connor smiles. "Good. It's a date." Then he hooks my arm through his. "For now, let's go kill it on the dance floor."

eleven

THE LAST WEEK has been pure torture.

I've seen Connor a lot in the office, but almost always around other people. As usual, our jobs have kept us pretty busy during the day and at night we have gone our separate ways—him to work on his manuscript and me to read and evaluate manuscripts that my assistant has pulled from the slush pile for consideration. (I know, I really need to get a life, right?)

We did manage to text a decent amount, mostly emojis and inconsequential stuff, and I have to admit that my flirty text game is definitely improving. (Kayla mentioned how proud she is that her confidence and dating lessons have paid off. I assured her that I still have a long way to go.)

Other than texting, I've had to satisfy myself with meaningful looks and winks across the boardroom table, one brush of our hands as he handed me my lunch out of the fridge in the break room, and one fleeting moment yesterday afternoon when he rushed into my office, closed the door behind him, leaned down to kiss me square on the mouth, and pulled back immediately, whispering, "I can't wait for tomorrow night" before hightailing it out of there again.

Essentially, I did *not* get enough of Connor Bryant this week. Not even close.

Which is why now I'm bouncing on my tiptoes on the stoop of Connor's modest-sized Chula Vista home as I wait for him to answer my knock. After a morning and afternoon that dragged on forever, the night has finally arrived and I've made sure to look my best while still keeping it casual in a pair of jeans, sandals, and a cap-sleeve black polka dot blouse.

For our first real date, Connor asked if he could cook me dinner—and hello, I've seen enough romcoms to know that if a man wants to cook for you, you say YES! Even though some women might prefer to be wined and dined at a fancy restaurant, I actually love that our date will be more low-key and out of the public eye—just me, him, and this bottle of red wine that I'm clutching.

Oh yeah, and his dog, Bruno.

When Connor opens the door, a golden retriever races out to attempt tackling me. "Bruno! Heel!"

The dog halts and looks up at me with mournful brown eyes. I laugh and squat to nuzzle him, allowing him to lick my cheek. "Good boy."

"What's it say that I'm jealous of my dog?"

I look up to find Connor leaning against the door frame, arms crossed over his chest. Standing, I take a step toward him and lose all train of thought, because how does a man make a black T-shirt and jeans look so good? "Hi." I hold out the wine.

He gently takes the bottle and tugs me into his embrace, giving me a kiss on the cheek—the one the dog didn't just lick, of course. "Hi. You look resplendent tonight."

I laugh and nudge past him, the dog following closely on my heels. My jaw drops as I take in his great room. It's probably the most stylish bachelor pad I've ever seen—not that I've seen a lot—with its high wood-beam ceilings, vintage leather furniture, velvet throw pillows, and a large piece of abstract artwork on the wall of the eat-in kitchen. "Wow, you really have a knack for decorating. Your place is lovely."

Some sort of heavenly scent wafts from the kitchen—garlic and oregano, if I'm not mistaken—which opens up into the room where we're currently standing. Even though it isn't large by any means, the stainless steel appliances, white shaker cabinets, and tile backsplash with a blue swirl pattern give it a luxurious air.

Either Connor makes more money than I do or he's able to save more than I can—possibly both.

He doesn't need the promotion like I do.

Nope. Not going there. Not tonight.

I clear my throat and pivot as he passes me into the kitchen and puts the wine on the counter. "Something smells amazing." Running my fingertips over the smooth wood of the countertop-height table, I then hang my purse on the back of one of the eight chairs.

"My mom's lasagna." Connor puts on potholders and leans down to pull a nine-by-thirteen dish from the oven. The cheesy air bubbles deflate as he removes it from the heat and places it on the island. "It's my go-to."

Oh. And suddenly, the whole thing loses a tiny bit of its luster. "For dates?"

He must notice the disappointment in my tone, because he turns, slips off the potholders, and walks toward me with such purpose that I retreat a few steps until the back of my legs hit his large couch. But then he places his hands on my shoulders. "Webster, I have never, in all my dating life, cooked for another woman."

"Really?"

"Really."

And before I can lift up on my tiptoes and show him how much that means to me—after all, cooking was the thing he did with his mom—he sweeps away again, back toward the kitchen, where he pulls a lidded bowl from the fridge. "The wine you brought will go great with dinner." He pulls the lid off the bowl, revealing a salad with bell peppers, cucumbers, and tomatoes, then points to one of the cabinets. "Would you get down a few glasses?"

"Of course." As we finish prepping dinner, he gives me an update on his manuscript. "I'm going to start querying agents."

"Yeah?" The wine falls from the bottle into the second glass, a stream of delightful purply red. "I'm so excited for you. Who are you going to query?"

We chat all things agents and editors as we sit down beside each other to eat the salad, lasagna, and garlic bread he pulled from the oven (which are all absolutely delectable, by the way). Then our conversation ebbs and flows across a variety of topics—from our favorite childhood memories to our favorite movies (his is *Braveheart*, and when I admit I've never seen it, he declares that we are totally watching it after dinner) to our ideal vacations (mine = reading on the beach, while his is hiking and staying at a mountain retreat, cuddled up with someone special while binge eating Reese's Pieces).

I can't believe how quickly the time has flown by when he serves cherry and almond crumble for dessert, and I lose myself in the pleasure of tasting the tart fruit mixed with sweet vanilla ice cream that he apparently made from scratch because *of course he did*. "I have one more change to make to your manuscript before you query."

His eyebrows lift as he pushes aside his empty ramekin. "And what's that?"

Using my spoon, I point to my last bite of dessert. "The hero needs to cook for the heroine."

"Is that right?" His hand inches toward mine, and a tiny thrill shoots up my spine at the contact—the way his thumb gently strokes the length of my forefinger.

"Yes." My eyes flick upward, and I lick my lips.

I've been waiting for his kiss all night—all week, because that little peck yesterday didn't count—and I wonder if it's finally going to happen.

But then he says something I don't expect. "You know, you're the only person in my life who would see my writing as a good thing."

"What do you mean?"

"My dad has made it very clear that the arts are not something he wants his sons to pursue."

"I'm sorry." And I sense he has something to get off his chest, so I squeeze his hand and wait.

That seems to be the reassurance he needs that, yes, I want to hear about his past. The good. The bad. The everything in between.

"I don't know if I've told you this or not, but my dad is a surgeon in Los Angeles. He wanted me to go into medicine too, like my brother did. I think he's always seen my job in sales and marketing as kind of ... I don't know. Disreputable." He shrugs. "Whatever his reasons, he's always acted like what I do isn't good enough for the Bryant name. So if he ever found out I wrote a book, that I want to be an author ..."

"Thus why you wanted to use a pen name."

"Exactly."

"But you've decided to use your real name anyway."

"Yeah. Screw him, right?" He says it light-heartedly, but I can tell by the frown lines around his mouth that he doesn't mean it. That he'd like nothing more than to be accepted by his dad for who he is.

"Maybe he'd be more accepting than you think."

"There you go, Evie. Always thinking so well of everyone." A bitter laugh ricochets from his throat. "But you're talking about the man who called his eighth-grade son a wuss for deciding to secretly try out for a musical instead of the basketball team."

"What? That's terrible."

"What's terrible is that he interrupted dress rehearsal and declared me an embarrassment in front of all my co-stars, then refused to let me participate in the show." His gaze is dark like a storm brewing on the horizon, one that's about to unleash a thousand pounds of water on your head. Not that I blame him. What kind of father does what his did? "After that, I committed to basketball so hard that I went full-court jock, got a scholarship, the whole she-bang. He was finally proud of something I did—and then I lost it all when I followed Victoria to Florida."

Ugh. "I can see why you don't think he'd be supportive of your writing."

"Especially since I write romance novels. I mean, how much more wussy can you get?" Suddenly, he stands. "All right, enough of my sob story. Ready to watch a movie?" Then he charges away from the table and toward the television. As he's getting *Braveheart* queued up, I clear the dishes from the table and put them in the sink to soak.

He turns off the lights and the room goes dark other than the blue glow of the TV. I sit on one end of the couch and am surprised at how comfortable it is.

Connor flicks a glance at me and sits on the other end of the couch. I'm momentarily depressed that he chose the spot farthest away, until he holds his arm out toward me. "I wouldn't mind some company over here."

He doesn't have to tell me twice. As he stretches out against the back of the couch, I lie down in front of him, the small spoon to his big spoon. His arm pulls me back against his chest, and my head rests half on the throw pillow at the end and half on the crook of his arm underneath me. Connor clicks on the movie and gives me a soft kiss on the neck before settling his chin on my shoulder. His breath glides past my collarbone, just under the lip of my blouse's collar, and it feels like an intimate caress with invisible fingers.

At first, I'm completely aware of every single place his body and mine are making contact. But as the movie progresses, I'm sucked into the story. And then I'm crying when love is lost, rejoicing when victory is had, and lamenting when it's over.

As he hits the Stop button, I shift toward him slightly so I'm on my back and he's angled just above me. "That was so tragically beautiful."

"Wasn't it?" One strong arm is still lying across my stomach, his fingers skimming my waist as he plays with the bottom of my blouse. "There were also some really cool fight scenes." His lips twitch.

"Right." I roll my eyes, laughing. "That too."

The whole room is quiet save a static buzzing from the still-lit television. This is my idea of heaven, just being in Connor's arms, being enveloped by the manly scent of his deodorant and shampoo, his golden-brown eyes watching me. I wonder what he's thinking.

But instead of asking, I absently trace his bicep tattoo —which is normally covered up—for several long moments. And then I realize that it's wisteria, the plant we stood under at the Friendship Garden. His mom's favorite flower. "Did you get this for your mom?"

"Yeah."

And my heart melts into goo at how much he loved his mother, how much he misses her, that he would memorialize her forever in ink on his body. "You're a sweet man, Connor Bryant."

"You'd better not tell anyone. It would ruin my reputation." He grins.

But instead of grinning back, the reminder of his reputation gives me pause. Makes me frown. Because there's still something I don't understand—something that makes me wonder if I'm once again trusting too easily.

I don't really think I am, but …

He cocks his head. "What is it?"

"Nothing." The thought is too embarrassing. I could never ask him outright.

Could I?

Surprisingly, he doesn't prod me further, just holds me while I process. The ceiling fan above us is turning and I become aware of a clacking sound that I didn't notice before, like it's slightly off-kilter.

I swallow, and my throat is as dry as the desert in a drought. "For years, I watched you flirt with almost every female in our office. I even heard rumors that you went out with several of them. That you …" I don't want to repeat what exactly it is I heard that he did with these co-workers, but let's just say it's not rated PG.

"Aw, Webster …" He sighs. "After Victoria dumped me out of left field, I kind of swore off dating. Not going out for drinks and hooking up afterward—real dating. I'm not proud of my actions, but it's the truth."

It makes sense and I'm glad he's being honest with me. "Thank you for sharing that. But …"

His brow creases and the hand that's holding my waist gives a little squeeze. "But what?"

"It's just …" I bite my lip. "You never flirted with *me*."

"You had a boyfriend."

"Not for the entire ten years that we've worked together." I pause. "I know that I'm quiet and quirky and make too many Jane Austen references and I've got nothing on the other women looks-wise—"

"Stop." His fingers leave my waist and find my lips, resting against them softly. "I'll admit, at first I didn't really notice you. I was a superficial jerk who was hurting and looking for a quick score."

I flinch as the brash truth hits me in the face.

But Connor continues, and I listen. "Then you said something in a meeting one time—I honestly don't even remember what—and it made me smile. And I started paying attention. You were always doing things to make others smile, Evie. You still are. And it was at that point that I also noticed what an incredibly stunning woman you are."

My cheeks go hot under his gaze. "So if you noticed me …"

"Why didn't I ask you out?"

I nod. I'm so pathetic, but I really have to know.

"Because instinctively I knew that you wouldn't be the kind of woman who would want a fling. You're the kind of woman who wants—and deserves—champagne and roses, not cheap wine coolers and dandelions that will blow away in seconds. I knew that I would just hurt you. So I didn't even let myself consider you as a possibility."

His words both thrill me and terrify me. Because what's changed? "And now?"

"Honestly?"

"Of course."

"I am still pretty positive that I'm not good enough for you. But ..." He smiles, shakes his head. "I like seeing myself through your eyes. I like seeing the world through your eyes. You're special, Evie, and ... I don't know. I guess I feel like maybe I finally could be the kind of man who hangs in there for the long haul. You make me feel that way."

Okay, I'm definitely glad I asked.

I reach my hand up and cup the side of his face where it hovers just inches over me. The stubble is rough against my palm. "Connor."

And before I can fully breathe out the word, his mouth descends onto mine. My lips part and I let my tongue dart out to taste him, to taste the lingering sweet cream from our dessert on his lips. He shifts so he's no longer beside me but on top—and as he presses me back against the pillow with his kisses, I can't help but sigh. Deeply.

Apparently, Connor likes this, because he growls and deepens the kiss. One of his hands is tangled in my hair, the other skimming the skin just under my shirt, along the top of my jeans. His touch is like wildfire—and it's spreading, containment zero percent, no water in sight.

I pull him as close as I can because I never want to know a world where Connor and I aren't this connected. He claims my mouth with his own over and over, then my neck, my collarbone, my shoulder.

Now it's my turn and I greedily angle my lips so I can reach the soft spot just below his ear.

When I take the very bottom of his lobe gently between my teeth, his hand flexes on my waist and he moans—like he's holding back but doesn't want to. "Evie." And then he's got his lips on mine yet again and there's no hesitation, no fear, nothing but pressure and passion and—

My phone rings.

And rings.

And rings, till I groan and stop kissing him. But he just moves his lips to my neck. "Ignore it."

So I do, till the ringing becomes so persistent that it makes me worried, effectively killing the mood. "I'm sorry. I need to check." And probably, I should come up for some air—let the haze of fiery desire fizzle off just a bit before we go farther than I'm comfortable with tonight.

He sighs and scoots away, tugging down his shirt, which got pushed up his torso sometime during our flurry. I blush at the disappearing wink of his abs then stumble to my feet.

Connor looks equally dazed, something akin to awe on his face. He scrubs his jaw as I hurry to the table where my phone rests in my purse. Fumbling around, I finally find the device so I can silence it.

But then my stomach drops. My mom has called ten times. There are ten voicemails.

And one text: *Call me ASAP. Dad had a heart attack.*

My world goes black as my shaking hand drops the phone.

twelve

· · ·

EVERY MUSCLE in my body hurts.

My bones too.

I shuck off my thick work gloves and lean against the wooden handle of my shovel, unable to move from the stall I've just mucked for what feels like the eightieth time. In reality, it's only been two and a half weeks since I came to my parents' farm in Iowa—two and a half weeks since we almost lost Dad.

The cool breeze blowing into the barn dries the sweat on my face and soon I'm shivering because it's only forty-something degrees outside. Cows low in the fields and I check the clock tacked to the barn wall. We already spent our entire morning doing so, but soon it will be time for Mom and me to milk them—again.

It's too much work for two people. I cannot believe Mom and Dad have been doing this by themselves all this time. No wonder Dad had a heart attack.

When I saw that text at Connor's place, I thought it

was over, that my Dad was dead or would be soon. I nearly collapsed but Connor was so patient and took charge, calling my mom and getting the details, then getting online and booking me a flight. And when he drove me home to pack a bag and then to the airport, he didn't say stupid platitudes like "it'll be okay, I promise" and "you're going to get through this"—because there's no possible way he could have known that.

Instead, he told me that since I'd watched *Braveheart* with him, we would have to watch *Pride & Prejudice* (my favorite) when I return. I still laugh at the memory of his jaw dropping when I informed him that the six-hour A&E version was the only one worth watching.

No, he didn't give me platitudes. Instead, he distracted me, because that's what I needed in the moment.

The fact he knew that … well, I won't forget it.

I set the shovel against the wall, bundle myself into the extra coat my mom loaned me, and look out across the rolling green prairie, where the nearest neighbor is two hundred acres away. Since it's only dinnertime, the sun hasn't even begun to set. But thanks to the cloud cover, it feels like it's eight o'clock at least.

Having lived in a place that perpetually smells like sun and surf for ten years, it always takes me a while to reacclimate to the very different aroma of a dairy farm. As I trudge toward my parents' white wood-slat house —the house where I grew up—I breathe in the long-ago familiar scents of fresh-mown grass and cow dander, somehow ignoring the stench of manure tinging the air (it's a superpower you obtain when growing up on a farm and thank goodness I haven't lost it).

I pull open the light green front door of my parents' house and am greeted by a wall of warmth and notes of spicy meat wafting in the air. After leaving my work boots outside, I take a quick peek into the small kitchen that looks like it belongs in the seventies (my parents' avocado-colored fridge has somehow survived all these years). My dad stirs meat in a skillet on the stovetop. His strong, broad shoulders have withered and shrunk in the last decade since I moved away, his hair is nearly gone, and his movements are much slower.

But I'm so, so thankful he's alive. According to my mom, he was unconscious for several hours before I arrived. And when I got there and grabbed his hand where he lay in that stark-white hospital bed, he just decided to wake up.

He looks up from his place at the stove, and the leathery skin around his eyes crinkles. "I hope you're hungry, Lynnie. I'm making tacos—your favorite."

I smile at his nickname for me—a shortening of Evelyn, my given name. "Thanks, Dad. Just going to wash up really quick."

"Let your mom know, will you? She said she was going to take a short nap, but that was an hour ago and I haven't seen hide nor hair of her since."

"Sure." My poor mom has been laboring even harder than usual, I think, and her hands aren't what they used to be. They sometimes swell up if she's worked an especially long day.

These are not things my parents would ever tell me, but I would have known if I'd been here.

Once I'm up the stairs and into my old room—where there's an embarrassingly large cardboard cut-out of Mr. Darcy from my high school days—I take a quick shower (it's my third one today because I can't stand to be so smelly at mealtimes). My hair fresh and smelling like strawberries, I walk down the hall and poke my head into my parents' room, but my mom is nowhere to be found. Maybe she went downstairs already.

As I'm turning to leave, something on my mom's dresser catches my eye. I know if she's put something there, it's meant to be private, but I can't ignore the black word I see flashing against the white paper: Past Due.

My fingers grab the paper and grip it as I read something else my parents have hidden from me. They're in danger of losing the farm.

But before I can freak out too much, there's a bump on the wall. Suddenly, I know where my mom is.

Inhaling a shaky breath, I put the letter down and go next door—to Janelle's old room. Mom is sitting on the edge of the twin-sized bed, hands in her lap, wearing the worn jean jacket she's had for thirty years, and she's got her eyes closed. Maybe she's trying to catch a whiff of my sister's long-gone peach body spray.

The whole place is a museum—from the 'N Sync posters on the wall to the *Tiger Beat* magazines on the bedside table, the paper now yellowed and curling. I step inside the doorway and run my fingertips over

Janelle's old boom box, where I know her copy of Alanis Morisette's *Jagged Little Pill* album is still loaded.

Grief is a funny thing. It's been nearly twenty years since my sister died, and yet whenever I enter the space that used to be hers, I'm taken down as if by a wave in the ocean. Like I've gone too deep, taken one step too many. If I'd just stayed on shore … but then I wouldn't know the sweetness of floating, of diving, of living.

So grief becomes a part of you, even when it's buried.

Right now though, tears fill my eyes as I watch my mom. For her, it must be even worse, living here where we got the news. Where we held the funeral. Where there's always a reminder of something—someone—missing.

I lower myself beside Mom and the bed squeaks. As if she knew I was there all along, Mom smiles, her eyes still closed, and slips her arm around my shoulders. Her soft gray-blonde hair presses against my forehead as she holds me.

And we cry, both of us, together.

Over Janelle. What we lost.

Over Dad. What we almost did.

And maybe she's crying over me too, what a disappointment I've been. How I left them to fend for themselves all these years.

Because if being back here has reminded me of anything, it's that they need me.

"Mom." My voice croaks as I straighten and turn slightly to face her, my right leg hitched up on the bed.

I don't want to admit I saw the notice, but we have to talk about it, don't we?

She opens her eyes and takes me in, smiling softly as she pats my knee. "You need to go home soon, sweetie."

What? Where did that come from? "I have weeks of vacation saved up that I haven't used, and Lisa said I could have as much time off as I need." Besides, does Mom really think I'm going to leave them in the lurch?

"But surely that boyfriend of yours misses you. I can see that you miss him."

I avert my eyes and run my hands over the purple comforter, which used to be dark but now is more of a lavender. "He's not my boyfriend." But we have Face-timed every single night since I've gotten here. He should have been using the time to work on his manuscript, but when I tell him that, he just tells me he'd rather be talking to me.

And who am I to argue with that?

"But you'd like him to be."

That elicits a smile. "Maybe." And by that I mean YES! Because at this point, seeing what care he's taken with me, remembering the look of awe on his face after we kissed, I know he's not who I thought he was.

There's a tiny part of me that's still worried he's saying what I want to hear, but Connor has never seemed the type to play the long game just to get a woman to sleep with him. And spending every night talking definitely seems like a long game to me.

That gives me hope.

So I can't deny I'm anxious to get home. Still, how can I leave? I tug at a loose thread on the coverlet. "You say I need to go home, but you can't possibly manage without me."

"Actually, I just found out this afternoon that your dad's disability insurance has kicked in, so we'll be getting some payments until he's fully recovered. Doc said about six months and he'll be right as rain—so long as I get him on a healthier diet and we can lower his stress."

Which will be really hard to do if he's working dawn to dusk like usual. But I can't deny that I'm relieved about the insurance. "That's really great, Mom."

"And it means you can go home and we can hire on a temporary worker—although it's been wonderful having you here."

"I've loved being here with you." Even though I've missed my job, housemates, California—and yes, Connor—the extra time with my parents has been oh so special. "But you should save that money to pay your mortgage, Mom."

She stiffens and I realize my error. But I can't take it back. "I wasn't trying to snoop, I promise. I just happened to see the notice in your room." I squint at her. "Why didn't you tell me, Mom?"

"It's fine. We're handling it." Mom shifts her gaze out the window, which gives a fantastic view of the lush green landscape for miles and miles. "We still have several options before we have to consider selling."

"Selling?" I practically shout the word. "You can't sell. This farm has been in our family for over a hundred years."

"True, but we're getting older. It's getting more diffi-cult to manage."

And you're not here to ease the burden.

I know my mom would never say the words—prob-ably doesn't even think them—but her voice reverber-ates in my head regardless.

"Just …" I take a steadying breath. "Don't sell yet, okay?"

"Evie, don't worry." She squeezes my knee. "I'm going to meet with the bank to discuss another loan soon. We'll figure it out."

"That's great. And I didn't want to tell you this—didn't want to get your hopes up—but I've got a promo-tion coming." I hope. "It pays a lot more."

"That's wonderful, Evie. I'm so proud of you." She tucks a piece of damp hair behind my ear. "I know Cali-fornia living is expensive."

"No, that's not … I mean, it is. But …"

Her wiry gray eyebrows lift. "You don't intend to give us the extra money, do you?" When I just squirm under her gaze, she shakes her head. "Oh, honey, we'd never ask that of you."

"You don't have to ask. I want to help. I'm part of this family too."

"Yes, but this is not your concern. You're borrowing trouble, love." My mother gathers me to her again, and she smells like peppermint—another scent of my child-hood. "We'll just take it one day at a time. It will all work out like it should. We'll get a loan or find some other way to survive. But don't waste your time worrying about us. Me and your dad, we're going to be fine. Have a little faith."

And in that moment—held by the woman I admire most in the world—somehow I do.

Somehow, despite being surrounded by my sister's things and the relics of the past, a peace like nothing I've ever felt winds its way through me.

Somehow, I believe that it will all work out.

Somehow.

thirteen

IT FEELS good to be home.

I pick up a pen and tap my foot against the carpeted floor of the Evermore conference room, where the editorial and sales teams sit in swivel chairs around a large oak table. Lisa is busy discussing the upcoming quarter, what projects should take front and center, what kinds of books are trending, what we need to look into acquiring for our next calendar year.

I like all of this high-level stuff to a point, but I am itching to get back to the 1870s western romance I'm editing.

Of course, my fidgeting has nothing to do with the man sitting across the table from me—the one whose chocolate eyes are devouring me, who keeps winking at me to see if I'll blush.

Since coming home from Iowa a week and a half ago, Connor and I have been spending every moment we can together—inside and outside the office. Of course, we both agreed to keep things professional in front of our co-workers, which means finding creative excuses for hanging out behind closed doors.

Doors like the one to the copy and fax room.

The supply closet.

This very conference room.

I bite down on the pen I'm holding to keep the tremor of some very good memories at bay. Even though his attention is now fixed on our boss, Connor grins like he can sense my thoughts.

"All right, team. That's it for now." Lisa claps.

Beside me, my editor Kelly—who has clearly been fighting the post-lunch coma—snaps to attention. She isn't the only one who has trouble with these three o'clock Wednesday afternoon meetings. If I hadn't met Kayla at Java Awakening for my daily americano, I'd be in the same boat.

As people start filtering out of the room, I turn to Kelly. "Late night?"

"Yes." She takes a swig of break-room coffee and grimaces. (I don't blame her. The coffee here is terrible.) "Gabby is teething and waking up ten times a night."

"Wow. I can't imagine." Because I really like my sleep. But also because I have no concept of what it's like to be a single mom to a ten-month-old—or a mom at all, for that matter. I wasn't really around a lot of babies or little kids growing up, but I've still always imagined myself with a decent-sized family. Three, maybe four kids.

I wonder if Connor wants kids …

Whoa. Where did that thought come from? I mean,

yes, my affection for him has grown immensely but we haven't even had the DTR talk yet (and yes, Kayla had to tell me that the acronym stands for "define the relationship"). If I don't know whether the man considers me his girlfriend, I shouldn't be thinking about having his babies.

Although, let's be honest. I wouldn't say no.

But right now isn't about Connor and me. It's about Kelly and what she's going through. I squeeze her forearm. "I'm sure that's stressful."

"It can be, but I'm figuring it out." She pushes back from the table. "I'm working hard to meet my deadline on the Delaney Smith project. It's just hard to think clearly when you haven't had much sleep, you know?"

"I get that." And it's on the tip of my tongue, to offer to step in. But Lisa's words bounce around in my brain. *"Sometimes you have to admit that you can't solve everyone else's problems. All you can do is be there for them, to support them."*

So I stand with Kelly and walk with her out the door. Before we reach my office, I turn. "I know you've got this. You're capable and strong and an awesome editor. Delaney is lucky to have you on her team."

A smile blooms on Kelly's lips. "Thanks, Evie. Your belief in me means a lot. I won't let you down."

"I know." I pause, chewing the inside of my lip. Because I know what it is to put on a brave face, to swallow the pain, to nearly drown from loneliness when a life vest was right there. And whatever Lisa says, I know in this moment, it's not about me trying to solve Kelly's problem. It's not about not trusting her. It's about supporting her in the best way I know how. "Keep me posted on your progress, all right? If it's getting down to the wire and you're coming up against some difficulties in finishing on time, we can work together to come up with some creative solutions."

Kelly presses a palm against her heart. "Thank you so much." Then she nods, straightens her posture, and walks down the hall toward her cubicle.

Nearly skipping, I head into my office.

"And *that* is why you'd make such a great associate publisher."

I whirl at the sound of Connor's voice. He's standing in the doorway, hands in his pockets, as casual as you please. I search for the humor in his expression, but there's none. He's serious about what he said, which is strange, because we decided a while ago not to talk about the promotion—not to let the competition of it ruin what was blooming between us. Whoever gets the job, the other will be happy for that person.

This is the first time he's ever acknowledged that I might be a good fit for the position. "You really think so?"

He nods, slow. "I've always thought you'd rather stay an editor, but you're really coming into your own with the management stuff. Not that you weren't a good manager before, but ..." Shrugging, Connor moves into the office and kicks the door closed behind him. "The old Evie would have let Kelly walk all over her, or at the very least, you'd have volunteered to do the whole project plus babysit overnight."

I smile softly at the exaggeration and step toward

him until we're toe to toe. "The old Evie?" I reach out and play with one of the buttons on his shirt. "You think I've changed?"

But I know I have. I'm different. For the first time, I feel desired. Beautiful.

Seen.

Looking back, I don't think David ever really saw me. But in a matter of months, Connor does.

"Or maybe I'm just getting to know the real Evie for the first time." He loops a hand around me, and goose-bumps slide along the back of my neck.

"Maybe …" I pause. Then I peek up at him, lower my voice. "Maybe I'm finally confident enough to come out of my cocoon." And it strikes me that maybe I really did fake it till I made it.

Has Evie Denmark finally, actually, arrived?

Connor pushes my hair behind my ear and his fingers caress my neck. "In my opinion, you make one heck of a gorgeous butterfly."

Then he kisses me, soft and slow, till I feel it all the way down in my toes. We've had plenty of passionate kisses, but this one—this one feels different, like he's telling me something he wasn't prepared to say before. Like he's had a secret and it's been blooming in his chest, but maybe, just maybe, he's ready to let it out.

But before he can, there's a knock on my door and we break apart just in time as Lisa sticks her head inside. Oh goodness, kill me now, because she's glancing between us and can probably see the guilt—the glow—written all over us.

I clear my throat. "Hi, Lisa. I was just, uh …"

"We were about to go over some promo ideas for the Landry series." How does Connor sound so smooth, so unaffected? But thank goodness one of us does because I'm about ready to start fanning myself. Did someone turn up the thermostat in here today? "Did you want to join us?"

Lisa crosses her arms, cocks her head. "No, thanks. I've got paperwork a mile high." She studies me, as if trying to suss something out.

Nothing to see here, ma'am. Everything is a-okay. Totally normal. Mmm hmmm.

Now I'm sweating through my shirt. Maybe we should just confess.

But before I get the chance to, Lisa waves her hand nonchalantly. "I just stopped by to see if everything was all right, Evie. You seem ... distracted lately." A quick glance between Connor and me leaves me in a near faint. But then my boss's features soften. "Is your father doing okay still?"

Blowing out a breath, I nod. "Great, actually. My parents hired a local college student to help out through the end of summer, so that's been fabulous." And although I can't help but worry about the finances, Dad's health, and everything in between, I have been trying to hold onto that faith my mom was talking about. "Even if it was hard for Dad at first not to work— he loves his job—I think he's been starting to enjoy his time off."

Connor's eyes are twinkling as I ramble and I want to wipe that smirk off his face. I have discovered his sides are quite ticklish, so I silently begin to plot my revenge.

If only Lisa would leave.

"Glad to hear it." She turns, but looks back, one eyebrow lifted. "I look forward to hearing these promotion ideas you two are discussing."

When she leaves, Connor starts laughing.

I nudge him. "She totally knows!" I hiss, because the door is still open.

"Because of you." He shakes his head, smiling. "You could never be a spy. You'd give up information like that"—he snaps—"if your interrogator even looked at you cross-eyed."

And then I'm laughing too. "Maybe we need to be more careful about our time together. Here."

He gets really close and leans down, and I think he's going to kiss me again—this time, with the door wide open. Not exactly what I meant by more careful, but at the moment, I'm rooted to the floor while he speaks. "If I can't kiss you again today, I'll go crazy."

I tilt my chin upward, exposing my lips, flirting with danger. I am not this girl—and yet, with Connor, I am. And I love it. "But you can't." I fake sigh, loud and dramatic. "Not here, anyway. So what are you going to do about it?"

He gets a wicked glint in his eye and bends even closer. My heart races at the thought that someone could stop by and our secret would be revealed. But I don't back away.

"Meet me here at five-thirty. We're going out."

Then he turns on his heel and leaves me standing here, lips practically puckered like a fool.

Somehow I manage to sit at my desk and work for the next hour and a half until it's time for our date. Just beforehand, I head to the bathroom to fluff my hair and reapply some of my makeup. When I step out, Connor is waiting by my office. He walks toward me. "Hey, Evie. I've got something to talk with you about. Mind if I walk you to your car?"

Of course, he's saying it for the benefit of the few co-workers still here this late. I stifle a giggle and reply. "I guess so."

He sticks his tongue out at me and this time, a giggle slips through my lips. Connor just shakes his head again, grinning.

We make our way to our cars and then to Suppannee House of Thai, where we order some delicious noodles. After eating, we hop into Connor's Lexus and he drives down Sunset Cliffs Boulevard until we hit a parking lot. Thankfully, there is a spot still available so we park and get out.

The cliff we are on drops drastically just beyond chains strung between wooden posts. Connor takes my hand and we walk along the top of the cliff, where people gather to watch the sunset happening in just a few minutes. The breeze whips my hair around as we maneuver through the crowd, down a path that leads us to an empty lower cliff jutting out into the vibrant ocean and staking its claim.

"This okay?"

"It's beautiful." I sit on the cold ground, with bits of

sand and rock scattered around me. Connor lowers himself just behind me, scooting forward until my back is settled against his chest and his arms are resting around me. Despite the chill in the air, I am warm and toasty—and exactly where I want to be.

I lean my head back, allowing the crashing sea and Connor's arms to lull me. The sun is edging itself below the horizon, producing a band of orange, another of yellow just above. It leaves the rest of the sky in this dreamy sort of haze that fills the entire space with a strange combination of darkness and light.

And we just sit there, taking it in, the world to our backs and the horizon ahead.

When the colors are diminished and the sun has said good night, I exhale and close my eyes. "What a perfect evening."

"Mmm," Connor says into my hair. And even though we've both been quiet for the last little while, I sense something in him—not his usual lightness. Something heavier.

Not necessarily bad. Just … deep.

"What's going on in that sexy brain of yours?" And when he doesn't respond with a quip, my suspicions are confirmed. I scooch forward slightly and turn so I can see him—as much as is possible in the dwindling light. "You okay?"

His eyes search mine for a moment before he says anything. "I was just thinking …" He blows out a breath and massages the back of his neck. "I heard back from two agents. They want me to send them my full manuscript."

"Connor! That's incredible." I grab his hands, squeeze. "I had no doubt."

"No, you didn't, did you?" And there's this funny look on his face, like he's surprised. "From the beginning, you have been my encourager, my cheerleader, my truth teller."

I suck in a sharp breath as he repeats back my own words from the Friendship Garden—the ones I used to describe a bookish heroine's role in a hero's journey. But the way he's looking at me is anything but fictional.

Connor threads our fingers together, lifts them to his mouth, and kisses them one by one, his eyes never leaving mine. "I'm falling in love with you, Evie Denmark."

Swoon! All of the romance novels I've ever read have fallen short of accurately describing this moment. The searing from the inside out. The fall so fast you're afraid to hit the ground. The rocket that propels you into space, a new dimension in time, a new stratosphere.

I bite my lip. "I'm falling in love with you too."

He pulls me onto his lap and does a much more thorough job of kissing me than he could earlier in my office. "So does this mean you'll be my girlfriend?"

"Um, yes."

"Good. Because, as my girlfriend, I have a huge favor to ask." He averts his eyes, almost like he's nervous. "I kind of have this family reunion this weekend. It starts on Friday night, goes through Sunday morning, and it's a long drive. I wasn't going to go, but my brother and his family are flying in from New York and he keeps bugging me to show up because we're also celebrating my grandma's ninetieth birthday."

"Do you need me to watch Bruno while you're away?"

"No, my neighbor is going to do that." He plays with my hair, twisting it gently around his fingertips. "I was hoping you might go with me."

"Of course I will." He wants me to meet his family! This is … everything. But then a thought occurs. "You weren't going to go because your dad will be there."

His brow darkens. "Yeah." He pauses. "Webster, you make me feel like anything is possible. Even … maybe, I don't know. Reconciling with him or something. But I won't have the courage to try without you by my side."

Oh, Connor. I set my forehead against his. "I'll be there every step of the way, for as long as you want me to be."

Because that's what you do when you love someone.

And I one thousand percent am in love with Connor Bryant.

fourteen

· · ·

I ABSOLUTELY LOVE Connor's family.

From his sweet grandma Doris to his crazy Uncle Marty to his brother and sister-in-law Kevin and Lola (and their two adorable children), they've been so welcoming, so friendly. And more than one have expressed their surprise—and delight—that Connor showed up with a date. Not just a date, but a girlfriend (a word I still internally squeal at upon hearing). Apparently, he hasn't brought a woman home since Victoria.

The reunion is at this amazing resort on a lake just an hour north of Fresno. Connor was right—it took seven hours after work yesterday to get here, and by the time we pulled in at midnight, we could barely keep our eyes open. The concierge directed us to our two-bedroom cabin and, after unloading our bags, we went to our separate rooms and crashed.

This morning dawned bright and early, and the view outside my window stole my breath. The lake sparkled like someone had shone a large flashlight on it, and it just beckoned to me. I threw on my jacket, walked through our adorably rustic living room (complete with a fireplace I fully intend to snuggle in front of tonight), and stepped out onto the back deck.

California has always amazed me. It can be beaches and city and sun and surf, but it's also mountains and pine trees and sparkling lakes. I inhaled the fresh air and listened to birds skittering and singing in the branches above me.

Then Connor woke up, and we got ready and headed to breakfast with his family, who has rented out the entire resort for the weekend. Between aunts, uncles, cousins, and grandparents, there are more than a hundred people here, ranging from Connor's grandma to Kevin and Lola's kids Ellie and Tommy. I met his dad briefly, noting the way Connor gave him a stiff hand-shake before turning to chat with a few of his cousins.

Now, after a day spent hiking around the lake with a group of thirty or so relatives, Connor and I are on a pontoon with about ten people, including Connor's brother and dad, who is clutching a Bud Light. (Lola stayed back at the resort so the kids could catch a nap.)

For a man in his sixties, Robert Bryant is still very handsome with his tan skin, full head of silver hair, and trim figure. He looks a lot like Connor, especially his nose and mouth.

But he doesn't have the same laugh lines that Connor does.

This is the first time I've spent more than fifteen minutes in Robert's presence, since he chose to stay behind for the hike. But I find myself fidgeting under his gaze as he studies me while Kevin and Connor shoot the breeze. We sit in a U-shape on the cushions at the back of the boat while Connor's uncle drives and chats with Connor's cousins—his sons.

"Man, work has been so stressful lately, so this is a little slice of heaven." Kevin stretches out and tugs his ball cap down. "How's work going for you?"

"You know. Same old." Connor's face is drawn, lips tight, as if he'd rather be getting an MRI than talking about this with his family.

I grab his hand, squeeze, a show of my silent support.

He glances at me, and even though he's wearing sunglasses and I can't see his eyes, I know he's flashing me a grateful look. Then he coughs, refocusing on Kevin —and his dad, whose interest has moved to him. "I enjoy what I do."

"You enjoy lying to people?" This from his dad, who takes another swig of beer. "That's what marketing is, right? Spinning a lie to fit your version of the truth. All so you can sell something—and trashy romance novels at that." His upper lip curls in disgust.

Hey now. Some of our novels may have steam, but I make sure they're anything but trashy.

Thankfully, his brother speaks up. "Come on, Dad. Lighten up."

"How can I lighten up when one of my sons has chosen a career in direct opposition to what I do?"

"What does my being a marketing director have to do with your career?" Connor's tone has deepened.

Ocean spray hits my cheeks, cooling them from the overhead rays of sun—and the heated battle of words. Land comes into view and I have never been more relieved to see solid ground.

"I help people for a living. You lie to them." Robert shrugs, as if what he's just said doesn't have the power to cut the last string of hope for a relationship strung between him and Connor.

"Books help people." I can't help my interjection. All three men turn their attention to me, eyebrows arched as I fidget with the drawstring on my shorts, and I continue. "In my lowest times, reading about other people's struggles helps me to not feel so alone. And getting swept away in a story is sometimes a blessed escape from the harsh realities of life."

"Well." Robert huffs, drains his Bud, and smashes the empty can with his hand. "It's not like Connor here has anything to do with that part of it anyway."

"A good salesman finds the people who need the product—who the product can help."

"Bah." Connor's dad waves his hand, dismissing me. "He should have been a doctor. We"—he indicates himself and Kevin—"help people. But Connor had to go off and do something embarrassing. I'd rather tell my co-workers and friends that he's a drug dealer than in marketing."

"That's enough, Dad." Kevin rolls his eyes. "Connor wasn't even going to come this weekend, but I convinced him that you would be civil."

"I am being civil! But what else can I say when my son chooses such a disgraceful career?" He laughs, and it's harsh and grating against my ears. "At least he didn't end up *writing* the books. Now that would be a true embarrassment."

Now Connor is gripping my hand so tightly I nearly cry out in pain. "You know what, Dad? I actually did."

His dad straightens. "What are you talking about?"

The boat's engine cuts out and I see that we are almost to dock.

"I'm an author. My book—a romance novel—is with a few agents right now." With every word, a throbbing vein in Robert's forehead gets more pronounced, but Connor either doesn't notice or doesn't care. He's on a roll now. "In fact, I'm hoping to be a full-time author someday."

He is? He has never expressed that to me. But his book is good enough. He is good enough.

And if that's what he wants to do, I will fully support him.

"You ..." His dad sputters just as the boat butts up against the dock.

Our escape is imminent. I can feel it.

"And"—Connor stands and hauls me to my feet—"I'm using my real name. So who knows? Maybe one of your co-workers will buy my book someday and discover your dirty little secret."

"What secret?"

"That you actually have two sons, not just the one you claim publicly."

I am hovering over a bed of cotton, my skin light, my hair fluttering. I am warmth and glitter and all the good things. And yes, I know I'm dreaming, but this feeling—of full acceptance, of brightness, of energy—is worth holding onto.

"Evie."

And someone wants me to let go. I frown, shake my head. "No."

"Evie." There's a poke in my side, and dreamland floats away as I open my eyes. The room is dim, with curtains drawn, but I can see Connor lying right next to me on his bed.

That's right. After his epic fight with Robert, we headed back toward our cabin. Connor was quiet—distant—the whole walk, but as soon as we got inside, he pulled me into a fierce hug. And I don't think he cried, but his deep shudders told me he wanted to. I let him bury his face in my hair while I rubbed circles on his back.

And then, he started to lead me to his bedroom.

When I hesitated, he shook his head. "That's not ... I just want to hold you."

So we snuggled together on the bed and he tucked me against him. "I want to do things right with you, Evie," he whispered in my ear. "Which means we take our time. There's no rush for anything more than this. I'm not going anywhere."

Oh, how I love this man, I thought. Then we lay there until I apparently fell asleep.

"Hi." He trails a finger down the side of my face. "I hated to wake you, but we'll be late for dinner if we don't get up soon."

I frame his face with my hands. "How are you?"

"Been better. But watching you sleep cheered me up a bit." He kisses the tip of my nose.

We stand and get ready for dinner, then head over to the main resort hall, which smells like a roast and mashed potatoes. It seems like most of his family is already here, because the place is crowded with some people sitting at large rectangular tables, kids running around playing a game of tag, and other relatives chatting in groups off to the side.

Lola and Kevin's four-year-old daughter Ellie comes running up to Connor. "Hunky Con-Con!"

He chuckles and swings her up onto his hip. "Well, if it isn't my favorite niece."

"I'm your only niece, silly." She makes a funny face and he makes it back. My stomach twinges as I picture Connor with our little brown-eyed children someday.

Am I getting ahead of myself? Well, if I am, it's only because the man invited me to a freaking family reunion and then had the gall to stand there looking adorably dad-like as he plays peekaboo with his niece.

Somehow, Lola finds us in the crowd. "There you are, Elle Bell. I told you not to run off." She shifts eight-month-old Tommy from one hip to the other. "Oof, this guy is heavy."

"Here, let me." And I, the woman who has held maybe two babies her entire life, take Tommy from Lola as if it's the most natural thing in the world. I clear the drool from his lips and tickle his belly, making him laugh, and his laughter is light pinging through me.

So is the look Connor gives me—he looks the way I imagine I did seconds ago when picturing us having a family together someday.

Sweet mother of pearl, I've got to stop thinking about making babies with Connor Bryant.

Cheeks warm, I shift my focus back to Lola, who is eyeing the two of us and smiling. "So, how was your afternoon? Did they sleep for you?"

"Yes, like the dead. Thank goodness." She raises an eyebrow. "I heard I missed quite the outing, though."

Connor frowns and then kisses Ellie before putting her down. "I'll be right back." He leaves me standing there with Lola and the kids.

"Poor guy." Lola plays with Ellie's braid before the little girl darts away again. "Much as I love him, it's not like Kevin is perfect. But Robert's always been so much harder on Connor. It kills Kev that the two guys he loves the most don't get along."

I run my finger through Tommy's soft curls. "It kills Connor too. I think he just wants to be accepted, you know? Like his mom accepted him."

Before Lola can respond, there's a shout from somewhere in the crowd and her neck swivels in that direction. "Sorry, looks like Ellie has found dessert before dinner has even started." She puts her hands out for Tommy, and I reluctantly give him up. "I'll look for you after dinner. You still need to give me all the deets about you and Connor." With a wink, she's off, leaving me grinning.

I stand on my tiptoes to find Connor and spot him talking with Grandma Doris. Despite being ninety years old, she's not a frail little thing, and her voice is strong and sure as I approach. "I just wish you and your father could bury the hatchet once and for all."

"Grams, don't you think I've tried?" Though I can't see Connor's face, I can hear the frustration in his voice.

"Not hard enough, obviously." Doris presses Connor's right hand between her palms. "Your mother would roll around in her grave if she saw the way you two treat each other."

He stiffens. "That's not fair."

I've almost reached them now, but it feels intrusive to interrupt. So I hang back, wondering if I should cover my ears. But judging by the looks and leaning of those seated in the immediate vicinity, I'm not the only one listening.

"What's not fair is life," Doris says. "Life took your mother too young. Life requires hard work, and even then sometimes our dreams don't come true." She's momentarily distracted by something behind Connor, behind me. "Ah, Robert, there you are. Come here."

Connor's dad shuffles forward to join their little huddle. "What is it, Mom?"

I really should turn away. But then one of Connor's cousins—Tiffany, maybe—pushes out the chair beside her and whispers that I should sit. Then she turns her attention back to the trio. Weakly, I sink into the chair.

Connor has turned and I can see his stony face as he regards his father. "Maybe we should talk about this in private."

Doris dismisses this idea with a wave. "It's good to have witnesses. When I'm dead and buried, the family will hold you accountable." Oh, she's good at heaping on the guilt, isn't she? "Robert, what will it take to resolve this feud between the two of you?"

Connor's hands are fists at his side. I long to go to him, to comfort him somehow. "Grams, there's no f—"

"Shh. Well, Robert?"

"Like he said, Mom, there's no feud. I just want ..." Robert wobbles a bit on his feet, but rights himself just as Connor is reaching out to do the same. "I want to be proud of my son. And the only way that's gonna happen is if he stops 'following his heart'"—he says this in such a mocking voice, I want to weep for my man— "and gets serious. Stop chasing women, stop chasing foolish dreams, stop being less than you're capable of being. Stand up and be a Bryant."

"And that means being a doctor, right?" Connor spits out the words.

"Connor," Grams warns.

"Sorry."

Even his dad has the decency to look a little bit contrite. His repentance is tiny, but it's there. "I suppose it's too late for him to go to med school at this point in his life. Kevin pointed out that Connor's job may be more prestigious than I thought. Even told me he was up for a promotion. And if he can actually follow through with that, instead of going off half-cocked like he did when he ran off to the wrong college chasing the wrong girl, then …"

The listening crowd seems to draw a collective breath.

"I'd be proud of him."

And then Connor's family is applauding and Doris is beaming and I want to shout at how wrong it all is— that they're asking Connor to put back on the facade he's had to wear his whole life in order to be deemed good enough.

I turn sympathetic eyes to my boyfriend. But instead of eyes full of fury, his are … hopeful.

My stomach sinks, and I pray he hasn't once again bought into the lie.

fifteen

. . .

"KNOCK, KNOCK." I push Connor's office door open and step inside.

He glances up from his computer and gives me a smile, but it doesn't quite seem to reach his eyes. "What's up?"

I smooth my hands down my skirt and move closer to sit in the chair across from him. It's Friday afternoon —five days after the disastrous end to his family reunion—and I'm about to leave the office for a long-awaited girls' night out with my housemates. Since getting home late Sunday evening, we haven't seen much of each other. Connor's been working on project after project.

I know I'm probably being paranoid, but I feel like I'm losing him. When we're together, it's like part of him is hidden away again. Or maybe he's just distracted. Either way, I miss him, and I hope that he'll loosen up a bit on our date tomorrow night.

"Just wanted to stop in and see you before I head out."

He's looking at his computer again, squints, frowns. Then he shakes his head and moves his attention back to me. "Sorry. What did you say?"

"You okay?" I lean forward, longing to reach out and grab his hand. But even though we're dating, we're still trying to keep it on the down low at work until we know who is getting the promotion. We don't want our relationship to affect Lisa's decision at all. But once she offers it to one of us, we will tell her and sign whatever HR forms we need to.

Since my parents are doing so well—their loan came through, hallelujah!—I don't need the promotion like I used to. But there's part of me that thinks I'd like to have it anyway. Like Connor said, I'm coming into my own and it's exciting to think about what I could do as an associate publisher. I've already got some great ideas for how to support the teams I'd be leading.

"Everything's fine." Connor shifts in his seat and tugs at his tie. "It's just that I heard from the second agent I submitted to."

I scoot to the edge of my chair. "The second one? What about the first?"

"Rejected."

"What? When?" And why didn't he tell me?

"A few days ago. It's not a big deal." But I can tell by his drooping shoulders, his chest caving inward, that it is a very big deal. "The second one just rejected me too."

"I'm sorry, Connor." Who cares what everyone else

thinks? I stand up and round the desk to give him a hug. But he's quick about it and then pulls away.

A tiny shard of doubt pokes me in the ribs. But maybe this is how he handles disappointment. Could be he just needs some time alone to process.

Chewing the inside of my cheek, I go back to the chair and stand behind it, gripping the back. "Did they say why?" They don't always. Sometimes you just get a form rejection, which I understand, considering I have to do the same thing due to the sheer volume of submissions we receive.

"Something about not having a platform or social media influence." He shrugs again. "Like I said. No big deal."

"If you want, I'll help you find other agents to submit to."

"I don't know. Maybe." He points to his computer. "Sorry, I've got a ton of work to finish up. It's going to be a long evening."

"Sure, no problem." My chest tightens. "Are we still on for tomorrow night?"

"Actually, I think I'll be working all weekend. Rain check?" There's a flicker of something in his eyes—regret?—and already he's back to facing his monitor.

"Um, sure. Call me if you get a break."

He nods while stroking his chin, reading something on the screen so intently I wonder if light beams are going to shoot out of his eyes.

Okay, then.

I shake out my hands as I leave his office, blood buzzing in my ears. Checking my watch, I move quickly into my office to collect my things. Even though I'm itching to figure out why Connor is freezing me out, girls' night is starting soon, and I can't bail like I did last time—the night of the earthquake.

So much has changed since that February day nearly three months ago.

When I step back into the hall, I pull up short at the sight of my boss coming toward my office. "Evie, good. I caught you before you left. Can we talk?"

"Um, yeah. Sure."

"Great." Lisa ushers me back into the office and shuts the door behind us. She moves the two chairs on the nearest side of my desk apart so they face each other. She sits in one and I take the other. "I'm sorry to be doing this at the end of the workweek, but I just got the final go-ahead from the board."

Is she about to say what I think she is? I press a fist against my thigh. "No problem."

"I'm pleased to offer you the associate publisher position. Congratulations, Evie."

My hand covers my mouth and I want to leap up and pump my fist. But just as quickly, I consider Connor —how this will make him feel. Still, I have to express my gratitude. "Thank you so much, Lisa. I … I don't know what to say."

Her head tips. "Ideally, you'll say yes."

"I'd like the weekend to think it over, if that's all right." I falter for the right words. "It's just a big decision. A big opportunity."

"I understand. But I want you to know that I've seen a tremendous change in you over the last three months.

You're more sure of yourself, more poised, and you've really helped your team to blossom. Instead of catching fish for them, you've taught them how to thread a worm on a hook and find their own dinner, so to speak." Then she shivers, gritting her teeth. "Sorry, that was a rather gruesome visual image. The point is, Evie, you've earned this, and I'd love nothing more than to have you beside me working to propel Evermore to new heights."

"Wow." It's all I can say, really. "Thank you. I'll let you know first thing on Monday."

"Wonderful." Lisa stands then sits again quickly. "There is one more thing."

She hesitates—and you know that feeling you get in your stomach when the hero and heroine in your favorite book are about to break up? You can see it coming before it even happens? That sick foreboding?

That's how I feel in this moment.

Then Lisa plows on. "I've decided that I'm going to let you take the subsidiary rights, marketing, and editorial departments under your wing as direct reports. I'll handle all the others."

I blink. "Wait. I thought …"

"The original plan was, of course, to ease you into this and only give you two departments, but you've shown such surprising growth that I'm positive it's something you can handle." She studies me so intently I begin to squirm like a cockroach under a microscope. "And you and Connor have been working so well together lately that I thought it would be a natural transition."

"S-so, he's going to be my direct report?"

"Yes, as will Jorge in subsidiary rights and whoever we promote to your position in editorial."

My head spins. I'm going to be Connor's boss. This is not good. Evermore has a very clear "no dating subordinates" policy. Very clear—as in, people have lost their jobs over it in the past.

"Is that negotiable at all?"

"I'm afraid not." I've never known Lisa to be cruel, but there's a question in her gaze. "It's not a problem for any reason, is it?"

She knows.

She totally knows.

Is she testing me or something? I don't want to lie. "Um, well …"

"Great." Lisa stands again, this time for good. "I'll be eagerly awaiting your answer on Monday." She strides to the door, then turns, her eyes serious. "And Evie, I do hope you won't let anything hold you back from saying yes. You've worked too hard and are too talented for that."

Then she whisks away and I can finally breathe.

Connor.

I have to tell Connor.

Snatching my purse again, I hurry to his office, where he seemed to indicate he'd be all night—but he's nowhere to be found. I try calling his cell but he doesn't answer, and I need to be getting to drinks anyway. Briefly I consider texting him, but this isn't something I want to discuss over the phone.

His car isn't in the parking lot, and I'm fighting the thought that he lied to me as I drive to the restaurant.

Maybe he just stepped out for some air, or to pick up some dinner. *This doesn't mean I'm losing him. He said he was falling in love with me. That means something.*

I drive to the nightclub-slash-bar in the Gaslamp Quarter that Kayla picked out for our little soiree and somehow find parking despite the downtown traffic. The boutique nightclub gives me all the glamorous vibes with its wooden accents, plush rugs, and beaded tiered chandeliers. In the place of tables and chairs, there are deep-set couches and overstuffed loungers arranged in semi-circles all across the main floor, which I cross to find my friends in a low-lit corner already sipping cocktails.

Kayla spots me and waves. "Evie!" She's clearly already a few drinks in because she's got her happy-drunk smile on. And when I approach, she leaps up and practically tackles me, wobbling on her five-inch spikes that are expertly paired with a slinky silver dress that hugs all her curves.

"Hey." I laugh, because a girls' night is exactly what I need after all.

My other housemates send their greetings from the red couch as I lower myself into one of the cream-colored armchairs. I note each of their drinks, which so perfectly represent their personalities. Alexis is drinking a gin and tonic, Shelby a glass of white wine, and Lauren what looks like a Sex on the Beach. There's an assortment of appetizers laid out on the low wooden table.

A server approaches and places a white square napkin on the side table next to me. "Can I get you something to drink?" Thankfully this isn't one of those super loud bars where she'd have to shout to be heard. There's just a light hint of music floating above the rafters, enough to sprinkle down on us but not overwhelm the conversation.

"Another cosmo for me." Kayla raises her hand from the armchair next to mine. "And whatever else these ladies want, on me. We're celebrating tonight!"

After I put in my request for a mudslide (because chocolate and coffee liqueur, hello!), I turn to Kayla. "What are we celebrating?" She can't possibly know about my promotion, so it has to be something else.

"Ladies, I paid off my student loans!" Standing, Kayla holds her arms over her head and shakes her booty. Three guys a few couches over nudge each other and smile appreciatively. "Which means, I could leave the Wicked Witch in the freaking dust if I wanted to."

"That's amazing." Once she sits again, I lean over and squeeze her elbow.

"So when's your last day?" Alexis consumes the rest of her drink and sits back against the couch. Her lime green hair glistens under the chandeliers.

"You know, the best time to find a new job is when you've still got one." Shelby takes a piece of bread from one of the platters, smears it with orange-colored jam, and places a slice of brie on top. My stomach growls as she oh-so-gently nibbles the end. "Speaking of new jobs, did I tell you all that Eric got one at my school?"

Eric and Shelby have been best friends for who knows how long. Infancy? We all think he likes her, but Shelby just softly laughs off our suggestion and says he knows better than to like her. Which makes no sense, because Shelby is the sweetest woman I know.

"Doing what?" I lean forward and snag a portabella fry, dipping it into some sort of green aioli before tasting it. Mmm. Cilantro and avocado dance on my tongue.

"He is going to be the middle school history teacher." Shelby teaches at a K-8 school, so this makes sense. "I'm so excited to get to eat lunch together every day."

Across the table from me, Alexis arches her green brow (because, yes, she dyes her eyebrows too). "Sounds … cozy."

Kayla snorts and Shelby frowns. But before she can protest, Lauren throws her arm around Shelby's shoulder. "It sounds amazing! Y'all are going to have so much fun."

Our server stops by with my and Kayla's drinks, plus three more. She points to the table of guys a few couches over from us, who lift their chins in the universal "how you doing" greeting. "These are compliments of your fans over there."

We thank her and lift our drinks to the guys, who fist bump each other. Then we clink our glasses all together.

Kayla sits back in her chair and directs her attention to me. Her drink sloshes a little as she leans forward. "So, Evs," she slurs. Wow. Kayla rarely gets this wasted (she likes to be in control). She must really be happy— or maybe, like me, she feels a little lost and this is her way of covering that up. After all, she's been so focused on paying off those loans that she hasn't thought much beyond this moment. To my knowledge, at least. "We all gave life updates before you got here. Your turn."

I nudge my finger through the condensation forming on the outside of my drink. "Just before I came, my boss told me she's giving me the promotion."

"What? Why didn't you lead with that?" And Kayla is tackling me again, this time while I'm sitting, so I'm guessing the guys who paid for our drinks are also getting a show thanks to her short dress. But my bestie isn't fazed one bit as she plops back in her seat.

My other friends are cracking up at Kayla's behavior and congratulating me and they're all diving into the food and their drinks as I tell them the story—first about the family reunion and where Connor and I were at as of last weekend. Even though Kayla knows all of this because she grilled me right when I got back, it's much easier to update the others as a group since we're rarely all together.

When I get to the part in the story where Lisa told me I'll be Connor's boss, Kayla grins. "That's hot."

Alexis swats Kayla's knee. "You're too drunk to know what you're saying. It's not hot." She turns her eyes back to me, somber. "It's probably not allowed, is it?"

Then I swallow and I'm suddenly crying and the women are shoving napkins into my hands as tears I have been apparently holding inside stream from my eyes. "I don't know what to do." I hiccup despite having exactly zero sips of my drink so far. "I mean, I think the job would be kind of cool, you know? But I like editing too. I'd be happy being an editor for the rest of my life.

And if having the job means losing Connor, then I don't think I want it."

"No man is worth losing a job opportunity, girl," Alexis says. "Men come and go, but your work is what gives you value." She looks at me meaningfully over the top of her beverage. "Mark my words."

Lauren shakes her head. "So what gives me value is helping size two women become size zeroes? I don't think so." She places a hand on her chest. "And you're so quick to discount love. Why is that, Lexi Lou?"

"Don't call me that." Alexis scowls and nurses her gin and tonic like a baby. "I'm just saying that Evie shouldn't compromise what she really wants for a guy. That's all."

"Okay, fine." Lauren tilts her body toward mine. "So Evie, what *do* you want? The job … or Connor?"

"Connor, of course." The answer is easy when she puts it like that.

I laugh, a weight lifted. Because, yes. Jobs may come and go, but Connor and I have something special. I love him, and I'm pretty sure he loves me. That love shouldn't waver just because we're having an off week.

Of *course* I choose him.

"Didn't you want this job originally to help out your parents?" Shelby crosses her legs and places her hands on her knee. She tucks her short blonde hair behind her ear. "Is that not a concern anymore in the long term, even though they got the loan?"

I shrug. "My mom asked me to have faith, and that's what I'm trying to do." It's true that I sometimes still worry about what will happen when the loan runs out, if the cows stop producing, as my parents get older.

But when I expressed the concern to Connor, he told me he'd help me figure it out—that we were in this together.

My mother's words from last month float back to me: *"We'll just take it one day at a time. It will all work out like it should. Have a little faith."*

Yes. I am choosing to have faith. In the universe, in God … and in Connor Bryant, the man I love.

sixteen

· · ·

LISA BLINKS at me from across her desk. "Are you absolutely certain about this, Evie?"

"Y-yes." I attempt a smile despite the ache of doubt pounding behind my temples.

Because Connor barely texted me all weekend. When I asked him if we could talk, he made up excuses—even when I told him it was important.

It's like he's ghosting me.

But it just doesn't make sense, not with what he said at Sunset Cliffs (*"I'm falling in love with you, Evie Denmark"*). What he said at his family reunion (*"I'm not going anywhere"*).

Things don't change that quickly.

Unless he didn't mean all of that in the first place.

My boss looks on, lips in a flat line, probably not unaware of my internal struggle since I'm terrible at hiding my feelings. I wanted to wait until I had talked with Connor before giving Lisa my answer, but she caught me on the way into my office at seven fifty-three.

"May I ask why you're turning down this opportunity?" Even though the woman is petite, she's intimidating as heck right now, with her red power suit and coiffed hair that she clearly just got re-highlighted.

Me, on the other hand? I spent the weekend with Mr. Darcy—all six hours of him—and have puffy eyes for days. And I'm pretty sure I gained five pounds from all the Ben & Jerry's I ate sitting on my bed and watching my laptop like a sad little Eeyore. "I just really like editing."

Pretty sure Lisa can see right through me as she presses her lips together. "I'm disappointed, but it's your decision."

"Thanks for understanding."

"Of course."

I make my way to her door when she stops me. "Evie?"

"Yes?"

"If you see Connor this morning, would you let him know I need to speak with him?" Her voice is crisp, issuing a clear challenge.

The veins in my head pump harder, shooting pain through my whole body. "Sure."

She's going to offer him the job. I need to talk to him before that happens.

Hauling butt down the hallway, I peek in Connor's office. He's not there, but his jacket hangs on the back of his chair so I know he's here somewhere.

I hear voices coming from the break room. Of course.

He's probably dropping off his lunch in the fridge, getting some coffee, maybe picking up a box of Reese's Pieces from the vending machine. My low heels carry me to the kitchen area, where our love story kind of began. The windows are all repaired now, and there's no trace of the blood from my feet, no broken glass.

But there is Connor, chatting with June—*back off, lady, he's mine!*—and they're chuckling about something as she pours coffee into the mug he's holding. When she sees me, she frowns and scampers off.

It's just him and me, alone at last. "Hey." I move forward, praying we aren't interrupted again. "Can we talk?" I point to the farthest table in the break room, the one by the window where a tree branch nearly impaled me three months ago (yes, I'm exaggerating, but I'm on edge, okay?).

He seems to weigh the decision as he takes a sip of his brew. "I have a few minutes, yeah." We settle into the hard plastic chairs and he sets his mug on the laminate tabletop. "What's up?"

I breathe in the sight of him—the bloodshot eyes, the unshaven jaw, the tie that's hanging slightly askew—and my heart breaks for him. "You okay?"

"Fine." He grips the mug handle so hard I wonder if it's going to shatter. "What did you want to discuss?"

Seriously? "What's with the tone? Just because you're mad at your dad and disappointed about your agent rejections doesn't mean you should take it out on your girlfriend."

Please let those be the reasons he's acting this way.

He has the decency to wince before sneaking his

hand into mine underneath the table. "I'm sorry. You're right. I've been a jerk."

"I'm here for you."

His lips wear a ghost of a smile. "I know." He squeezes. "So what did you want to talk about?"

This is it. I pray the news that I got the job won't hurt his ego too much. "Lisa offered me the associate publisher position."

His hold on my hand loosens, but he keeps holding on. "Oh, yeah? That's huge." He looks away, clears his throat. "I'm happy for you."

Yeah, about as happy as Georgiana Darcy when she finds out Wickham's true intentions. "Here's the thing. Lisa told me that she changed her mind about the reporting structure. Both the editorial and marketing department heads will be reporting to the associate publisher."

Connor's head jerks back and his hand slips out of mine completely. "So, you're my new boss?"

The vending machine hums in the corner.

"No."

His nose crinkles. "I don't understand."

"I turned it down, Connor."

"What? Why?"

Doesn't he understand? "Because you know the rules as well as I do. Bosses can't date their subordinates."

Connor stares into his mug. And when he finally looks up at me, I don't recognize the coolness in his eyes.

Actually, I do. It's the way he used to regard me

—before.

"You shouldn't have done that, Evie." He pauses. "I wouldn't have."

My stomach clenches and my migraine nearly has me losing my breakfast. "W-what?"

And of course, it's at that exact moment that Lisa walks into the break room. I swipe at my cheeks, which I suddenly realize are wet.

"Connor, a word?" she says.

"Yep." Grabbing his coffee, he pushes away from the table and leaves with Lisa.

And I just sit there, head in my hands, shaking, for I don't know how long.

Eventually, two members of the marketing team filter into the room seeking a coffee fix. "I wonder who they'll promote to marketing director now that Connor's the associate publisher."

The words stoke a fire over the coals in my head. I want to scream. Instead, I stand on shaky legs and make my way to Connor's office, where two of his employees are chatting with him in excited tones about his promotion. Their backs are to me but I can hear every word.

One flips her long blonde hair over her shoulder. "Drinks at the Den this afternoon, right?"

"Ooo, yes! We have to do that." The other, a redhead, swivels her tiny waist and claps like she's a cheerleader in a high school movie.

"I'm not sure I'll have time. There's a lot to do here."

But the women simper and cajole until he concedes. "All right, if that's what the team wants to do."

"Congratulations." The word croaks from my throat, and all three of them spin to find me there.

"Thanks, Evie." He ducks his head. "Jess, Monique, I need to talk with Evie for a minute. Do you guys mind?"

They shake their heads and leave.

And I just stand there, arms crossed over my chest, staring at the man I love. "Well?"

"Come on, Evie." Connor leans back against his cluttered desk. "You didn't want the job. You're happier as an editor, anyway."

"I don't care about the job. What about *us*? We can't be together if one of us is the boss. That's why I turned it down."

He toes at something invisible on the ground. "Proving once again that you are too good for me. It was a pipe dream, you and me, and it's better we realize it now."

I don't accept that excuse. "You said you were falling in love with me."

"Well, I say a lot of things, don't I? Isn't that who I am? The sleazy salesman who will say whatever it takes to get what I want."

He doesn't mean it. He can't mean it. "Then what about what you told your dad? That your real dream is to be a full-time author someday? Are you also giving up on *that* completely?"

"Someday is for fools." His cheeks pale, Connor runs his fingers down the length of his tie. "Grams was right. Life isn't fair and it's time I learned that. My only regret is that I led you on. For that, I really am sorry."

But he doesn't look sorry. The mask he's wearing is like stone, like if I took a chisel to it, it would break into a thousand pieces. "Why are you doing this?" My voice trembles and I wish for once that I didn't wear my heart on my sleeve.

Because it breaks too easily that way.

"You want too much from me. For me to be something I'm not."

"No, I don't." I take a step toward him. "Unlike your dad, I just want you—who you really are, not this veneer you're putting on."

"The man you think I am, he's not real, even if we both wanted him to be. He's a lie. You're just too naive to realize it."

His words are a knife in my chest. He knows—knows!—my insecurity, how afraid I am to trust in the wrong person.

And he's using it against me.

Which means, in fact, that I *have* trusted the wrong person.

Again.

At the very least, I've given my heart to someone who doesn't really want it. Who doesn't love me as much as I love him.

Again.

When will I learn? And maybe that's the point. I won't.

I can't.

I trust blindly and I love bigger than I should and I'm blinded by this preconceived notion that everyone has good in them—if only someone would believe in them.

But I'm wrong. So very wrong.

Squaring my shoulders, I lift my chin. "You're right. I was an idiot to think you could ever be anything but a selfish ladies' man."

Then, ignoring his grimace, I turn on my heel and leave.

I can't be Connor's underling. Not anymore.

One week of that nonsense has been more than enough.

Staring at my computer screen, I scroll through the editorial job listings. There are several proofreader, news editor, and copywriting positions based in Des Moines, but that's still a few hours away from where my parents live. If I'm going to move home, I'd like to be close enough to lend a hand with the farm chores.

But beggars can't be choosers, I suppose.

I close the laptop lid and rub my dry eyes. I've been in here for hours while my roomies hang out together in the common spaces on their day off from work. They're headed out to a Memorial Day BBQ on the beach soon and I know they'll try to drag me along. Kayla especially thinks it will be good for me, to get out of my head, to forget for a little while.

Doesn't she realize I can't forget? That I thought Connor was *it* for me? My Mr. Darcy?

And now, he's acting as if I'm just another employee. Interestingly, he's no longer a flirt. He's all seriousness and brooding frowns, and even when women throw themselves at him, he's cold. Professional.

It's like all the light has gone out of his eyes. I wish I could shake him enough to get it back. But anytime I went near him this week, he drew back like he expected an assault (or at least a verbal one).

I thought the breakup with David was bad, but having to work with Connor—*for* Connor?

It's so much worse.

Sighing, I finally climb off my bed, stretching my sore leg muscles before venturing into the hallway. I can hear the TV blaring and my friends' laughter from the living room, and I just can't do it.

I need fresh air.

So I go back to my room, tug on my tennis shoes, grab my phone and keys, and sneak out through the garage door so I don't have to say no to Kayla when she inevitably asks to tag along.

There's a slight breeze as I exit the garage and head down the sidewalk. I nod hello to a few neighbors who are walking dogs and strolling by with kiddos, everyone enjoying some of the best weather California has to offer. The morning haze had burned off, leaving a gorgeous azure sky without a single cloud.

My phone rings from my back pocket. I'm tempted to let it go to voicemail, but a really stupid part of me wonders if it's Connor.

But it's Mom. She's been calling every day to check on me, and she'll only call back if I don't answer now.

"Hey, Mom."

"How's my girl today?" And before I can answer, she's launching into a diatribe about the cows and what a handful they are but how she loves them so. I know she's only trying to perk me up, make me laugh, but I just don't have it in me today.

Besides, I need to tell her about my decision. The one I made last night, after yet another sleepless night. I know two a.m. probably isn't the wisest time to make life-altering decisions, but really I'm just doing what I promised my parents I'd do ten years ago. This is the very antithesis of a last-minute decision. "I'm coming home, Mom." I sidestep an older couple that's taking a leisurely walk, holding hands. "As soon as I find a job in Iowa, I'm moving home."

"You really don't have to do that. Your dad and I are fine."

"But I want to."

Mom is silent for a bit as I wander the streets of my neighborhood. Before I understand where I am, I stop in front of the bungalow—the one Kayla told me was for sale more than three months ago.

Somehow, it's still on the market.

My heart leaps, but only momentarily. Because this place—the bungalow, California, Connor's arms—are not for me. Not anymore.

Iowa is calling my name. It's been calling my name for years, and I'm finally yielding to it.

"Evie."

"Yeah?"

There's a heavy huffing on the other line. "The worst thing that's ever happened to me is losing your sister."

My stomach crumples and I can't hold myself upright anymore. I sit on the edge of the sidewalk in front of my bungalow.

No. Not mine.

"Me too, Mom."

"I know, sweetheart." A pause. "But any clue what the second worst thing is?"

"Dad's heart attack?"

"Losing you."

"I'm sorry I left Iowa." A row of ants scampers along the warm white concrete at my feet, just beside the asphalt. I don't know if they're coming or going, but at least they have a destination. A solid purpose. I'll have that again soon. "But I'm coming back just as soon as I can find a job."

"I'm not talking about you moving to California."

Huh? "What then?"

The air seems to tighten between us, a band that reaches out through the phone and grabs hold of my lungs, anchoring Mom and me together. "Before the accident, you were such a happy-go-lucky child. So friendly to everyone, always chattering like a little blue jay, always spreading cheer. But when Janelle died, you lost your song. You turned inward and lost your ability to trust other people unconditionally."

I swallow as I use my foot to nudge a discarded chunk of bread into the path of the incoming ants. "Not all people."

"True. Men, then."

"Not Daddy."

"You know what I mean."

The lead ant grapples with the food, which must be a few hundred times its size, until a few more join in the struggle. Together, they lift the burden and work their way back to their little hill.

"It's not really the men I don't trust. It's myself."

"Aw, honey. You cannot let a couple bad apples ruin the whole batch. Just because a few sorry excuses for human beings took advantage of your generous spirit—your loving heart—doesn't mean *you* need to change."

I let that simmer for a moment before voicing my thoughts. "There's something wrong with me, Mom. Apparently I wasn't born equipped with bad-guy radar. I can't tell the difference between heartfelt words and those meant to charm me so others get what they want. And the result? I get hurt—or someone else does."

"I've told you a million times and I will tell you till I'm blue in the face, but Janelle's death was not your fault." Mom sighs. "I wish I could take away the hurt, baby. All I know is that you are beautiful and kind, and you have every reason to be confident in who you are. We all make mistakes, sure, and for better or worse, we learn lessons from our experiences. But sometimes those lessons are lies straight from the pit."

I push a hot tear from my cheek. "I don't know what's a lie and what's the truth right now."

"Love is always the truth, sweetie. Getting hurt is hard, but even harder would be a life without love."

And why does my stupid brain still think of Connor

when I hear the word *love*? I press a hand against my heart. "He doesn't love me, Mom. And I can't …" I inhale a trembling breath. "I can't stay here and be his direct report and see him day in and day out. Just one week has nearly killed me."

"I didn't raise you to be a quitter, Evie Denmark." Mom's voice softens. "And before you go quitting the job you love and running away to Iowa, think about what you want. Not what Dad and I want you to do. Not what your boss wants you to do. Not what Kayla wants you to do. What do *you* want?"

"I want to rewind the past few weeks to before I got offered the promotion. Before Connor's family reunion. Maybe even before we got together." Standing, I dust off the bits of sand from the backs of my legs. "I just want to be happy."

"Well, the first thing is impossible unless you've discovered time travel. But I think the second is very much within your abilities, if only you'll let your heart guide you. Trust yourself, Evie. Pray, ask for wisdom from those you love, sure—but ultimately, you're the one who has to live your life. Happiness is not a place. It doesn't happen *to* you. It's a state of mind, a choice. So choose happiness, my dear girl."

"Thanks, Mom."

After a round of *I-love-yous*, we hang up. Then, with her words playing on a loop in my head, I let the midday sun warm my bare arms and pivot slowly on my heel until I'm facing the bungalow again.

Choose happiness …

I can't choose how others react to the love and care I

show. I can only choose my own actions. And I don't want to hold back who I am. I don't want to be the kind of person who acts from a place of fear.

Not anymore.

And even though it scares me, I know what I need to do.

After pulling my phone from the back pocket of my jeans, I type out a text to Connor.

You once called me your truth teller, so here are some truths:

You are no longer the kind of man who chases women. You're a one-woman man who made me feel more beautiful, more cherished, than anyone has ever made me feel in my life.

And whatever you say, I know it wasn't a lie.

You are not chasing foolish dreams. You are building a solid future one brick, one story, at a time. Even if you never succeed at being an author (and I know you will), no one should mock you for going after something with all your heart.

I should know, because I've been stopping myself from fully giving my heart—I just didn't know it.

And yes, I did give my heart to you, but some part of me held back out of fear.

Here's that part: I love you, Connor Bryant.

And I'm not ashamed that I gave you my heart, because even if we can't be together, I know I gave my heart to a good man who was more than enough for me just as he was.

That being said, because I love you, I have to resign from my position at Evermore. And not so we can be together, but so I can move on.

Consider this my resignation, although I'll write a more formal one tomorrow.

I wish you all the best in your new job and in whatever you choose to do. Run hard after what you want, because you deserve it.

After all, you have quite the pulchritudinous soul. :)

All my love,

"Webster"

After a quick read through, I press Send and hurry back to my room, climb on my bed, open my laptop, and change the location on the job search website from Iowa to San Diego.

seventeen

. . .

IT'S my last day at Evermore.

My heart quakes as I step off the elevator, a few broken down empty boxes tucked under one arm and a Java Awakening latte in the other hand. The last two weeks, I've kept my head down, finished up projects, met with my team (who were surprisingly teary-eyed about my departure) to discuss their upcoming deadlines, and interviewed for my replacement (Kelly has actually stepped up to the plate in a major way and will do fabulously).

Other than a few days I've chosen to work from home, I've mostly stayed in my office, and Connor has stayed in his.

He hasn't said a thing about the text I sent nearly two weeks ago. Maybe he didn't even receive it.

Part of me wants to ask him. Get closure, you know? I stop just outside his office, but the light is off. Guess closure can wait.

I flip on the light in my office and step inside, inhaling. So this is what ten years of blood, sweat, tears, and laughter smell like—ink, paper, and old coffee in a mug I forgot to wash out yesterday.

The morning goes by quickly as I tape the boxes and start to take down everything I've accumulated in my office. Office mates stop in to wish me well, asking what I'll be doing next. I tell them for now that I'll be freelance editing, but I've got a few interviews at other publishers in the area. I tell them to look me up.

I tell them that I'm fine.

And except for the part of me that misses Connor terribly, I am.

I'm choosing to be. I'm making my own happiness, not letting the actions of others tear it away. It's a struggle minute by minute, but I'm doing it.

I pick up a photo of Kayla and me off the desk. We're at a cheap dive she found on the Internet, holding up drinks with these ridiculous feather boas around our necks. It was right after she passed her bar exam and got a job offer with the Wicked Witch. Little did she know how that would turn out. And for some reason, she's sticking it out there even now, when she could leave. Meanwhile, I'm leaving the job I love.

But we each choose our own happy, right? Mine consists of finding a new job and buying my own place when I have a down payment ready. (I'd love to buy the bungalow, but I'm not sure how it's stayed on the market this long, so my hopes aren't high in that regard.)

All that to say, I'm moving forward with faith that it'll all work out, just like Mom told me to do.

When the whole office is packed up, I tape the second box shut and plop into my chair. I'm going to miss these four walls—even my cracked ceiling. This place isn't perfect, but it's been my home.

And now, there's nothing left to do but go get that closure.

I take a deep breath and walk down the hall. But despite being eleven-thirty, Connor's office is still dark.

Unbelievable.

He's not coming in for my last day. Apparently, I didn't even matter enough to him to warrant a goodbye.

Slumping against the wall, I fight back the tears. *No.* I will not let him steal my happiness.

Just then, Lisa emerges from her office. "Evie, good. I need to talk with you." She was on vacation for the last few weeks. This is her first day back in the office and the first time I've seen her since putting in my resignation letter.

I squeeze my hands into fists at my sides. Release, squeeze, release. "All right." Following her, I take a seat in her office for probably the last time. She's been a wonderful boss, and I want her to know that. I was saving this speech for the afternoon going away party my team is throwing me in the break room (probably just cake and balloons, but that's plenty), but it wells up in my throat and forces its way out.

"Before you say anything, I wanted to let you know how much I appreciate you hiring me in the first place."

Lisa reclines her chair and fiddles with a pen as I talk.

"Here I was this totally green English major from cow country, fresh out of college, and you took a chance on me."

"I have always prided myself on being a good judge of character. I knew I'd found a winner in you." Her voice is soft. "I couldn't be prouder of you. And I don't want to lose you. In fact, that's why I called you in here. I have an offer for you—one I hope you'll accept."

I straighten in the chair. "What do you mean?"

"I had barely trudged into the office this morning when Connor stopped by saying he needed to talk to me."

"C-connor?" He was here? When? Must have arrived after I did. But then why is he gone again?

"Yes." She clicks the pen in and out. "Seems he tried to reach me multiple times on vacation, but Craig took me on a surprise cruise for our anniversary and begged me to put aside my phone and forget about work for a while. It was wonderful to get away from everything. Hard at first, but wonderful all the same."

"I see." But I don't. Why would Connor try to get ahold of Lisa during her vacation?

"Evie, he quit."

"I'm sorry, what?" My chest is squeezing, my blood rushing so fast in my veins that I wonder if I'm having a heart attack. Can thirty-two-year-olds have heart attacks? "I don't understand."

She snaps her chair forward so her elbows are leaning on the desk. "He put in his resignation. As of eight-thirty-two this morning, he no longer works at Evermore. And he told me in no uncertain terms that I had to use this opportunity to convince you to stay."

"Wait." I'm still processing, and yes, I'm slow, all right?

If Connor quit so I could have the job, it means he gave up money and prestige for me. And if his father ever found out that he'd sacrificed such a lucrative promotion—and for a woman at that—Connor would never earn his respect.

And I thought his dad's respect was what he wanted more than anything.

"Why would he do that?" The answer that's been stuck in my throat finally snaps loose.

Lisa's smile is stretched, her attempt at being patient with me even though she's probably frustrated that I don't get it. But how can I get it? This has come out of left field.

"I suspect it's because he loves you."

My head rears back and I look at her. She's not joking.

I shake my head vigorously. "He told me he didn't."

"Then his words and actions don't line up." She shrugs. "People don't give up a good job in this economy unless they're in love."

She's talking about me.

She's talking about me … and Connor.

Her jutted chin dares me to contradict her.

I can't talk. My brain is short-circuiting. The room swims as tears fill my eyes. "It doesn't make sense. It isn't rational."

"Love rarely is."

Love.

And like a gentle breeze, our conversation from that day in the Friendship Garden comes back to me, piece by piece. *"The hero needs to sacrifice for the heroine in such a way that they can be together in the end."*

Is that what he's done?

Oh my gosh, maybe he *does* love me.

I stand abruptly, nearly hitting my knee against the top of Lisa's desk. "I … I have to go."

"So is that a yes about the position?"

Biting my lip, I nod. "Yes. I think so. I … I need to talk to Connor first."

"Then go." She shoos at me. "I'll let everyone know the party this afternoon is off."

"Thank you." I scurry out of there, grab my purse off my desk, and then I'm in my car, calling him.

He doesn't answer.

But I know where he is.

When I reach the Japanese Friendship Garden, I leap from the vehicle and run down the path in my flats and cotton skirt. (It's one I buried in the back of my closet and wouldn't let Kayla toss because it's like wearing a blanket on my thighs and that's what I needed today, okay?)

I toss money at the ticket agent (okay, not really, but I do buy a ticket as quickly as humanly possible) and race through the crowd that's already much thicker than orange juice pulp.

I round a corner and there he is, standing under the wisteria—blessedly alone.

Stopping, I just stare at him and take him in. He's wearing a baseball hat, shorts, a T-shirt—everyday clothing, but on him, they take my breath away.

Fine, *he* takes my breath away, and it's got nothing to do with his manly arms or chiseled face or a body that looks like it's been sculpted by Phidias.

What draws me to him, what draws me forward, is the peace that's radiating off of him, the way he's lifting his face upward, eyes closed, his lungs filling and emptying in gentle waves—like he's finally free of something.

My shoes crunch on the pebbles underneath and his eyes fly open. He blinks. "Evie?"

"Hi, Connor." I continuing walking until we're together in the shade of the floral overhang.

He lifts his hand as if to test my realness, then drops it. "How did you find me?"

"I just talked to Lisa," I blurt. "And I just knew where you'd be. Because I know you. The real you. The one you hide from the world. But I see it."

Connor looks away for a moment, clearing his throat. Then his gaze sweeps over me and I feel swallowed by it—in a good way, like standing in a high-pressure shower that's washing away the grime of the day.

"I'm sorry for everything," he says. "I shouldn't have let my family get in my head. I just thought …" His jaw clenches. "It doesn't matter what I thought. It wasn't an excuse for how I treated you. And I know that it's probably too late for us, but I wanted you to stay at Evermore. It's where you want to be."

A few petals of the wisteria drift down, rustled and nudged by the breeze. "And what about you?"

He sticks his hands in his pockets. "I've got a few applications in at some marketing firms. But I've been writing, a lot actually." A sad smile crooks his lips. "Turns out it's a good outlet for heartbreak."

I brush the fallen flowers with the toe of my shoe. "Why is your heart broken?" Because though this feels like some sort of closure, that's not what I want anymore.

Not if there's a chance for us still.

"Don't make me say it, Evie."

But I'm not letting him off that easily. I move until we're toe to toe, and I reach out to touch his forearm. "I need you to say it, Connor."

"I got your text, and you have no idea what you did for me." His hand leaves his pocket and finds mine. "I didn't reply because I don't deserve a second chance with you. But I knew that the best thing I could do for you was give you back the job you rightfully earned and leave you in peace."

"That assumption was erroneous."

"Aw, Webster." He chuckles. "I'm going to miss all of those big, fancy words."

But I grind my foot into the ground. It's time to go big or go home. "Don't you get it, Connor? You're the hero in this love story of ours. I don't want another one."

"But you deserve the best."

"How about you trust *me* to decide what's best for me, huh? I choose you, Connor, and no one else will do." Then before he can protest anymore, I throw my arms around his neck, pull his head down, and kiss him.

Go, Evie! Go, Evie!

I pull my head back and laugh at my internal cheer-leader. But taking my future in my hands—quite literally, as I run them through Connor's hair—has never felt so good.

"Evie Denmark, you're the most pulchritudinous thing I've ever seen." He's looking at me, complete awe and love written all over his face as his arms hold me tight. "An earthquake may have brought us together, but you're the one who has rocked my world completely."

"Ooo, you should be an author or something." I grin. "Because that was quite the line."

"There's plenty more where that came from."

"And what about an HEA?" I ask. "Is one of those in store for this hero and heroine?"

"You'd better believe it."

And as he kisses me, I do.

epilogue

. . .

Kayla

THE WICKED WITCH has taken it one step too far this time.

I add an extra stomp to my step as I fling open the door of Java Awakening and march to the counter. The lingering scent of baked goods and strong espresso envelops me. Thank goodness there isn't a line, because I'm not sure I could stand behind any Slow Sarahs or Indecisive Isaacs today without being rude.

Josh is wiping down the counter with a wet rag. His eyebrows arch when he sees me.

Placing both of my hands on the counter and exhaling rapidly (I wonder if a human can breathe fire?), I lean in. "I'll take the largest caffè mocha you can make. Extra chocolate. Extra whipped cream."

He saunters to the cash register as slow as you please and rings up my order. "Rough day?"

"You have no idea." I hand over my credit card. "Have you ever been so mad at someone that there's like, a raging inferno in your stomach? And even though you want to scream and let loose every curse word you know, all you really can do is smile and nod?"

"Can't say that I have." The corner of his mouth twitches, like he finds me amusing. I'm glad someone does.

"Well, you're lucky." And now I just feel like a petulant toddler. But can I help it that my boss—aka Miranda, aka the Wicked Witch—inspires such rage in me? You'd think that as the only two females in our office, we'd be banding together. But nope. Instead, she is always finding new ways to undermine me in front of the guys.

Like today, as everyone was exiting our conference room, when she told me very loudly—so the entire team could hear—that my outfit did not comply with the office dress code.

So much for an unspoken sisterhood.

Guess it's every woman for herself.

"Do you think my dress is too sexy?" I blurt the question because I just really need some validation here.

Josh fumbles my credit card as he attempts to hand it back to me. "Um …"

"For work. Do you think there's anything inappropriate about my outfit?" I sweep my hands from my armpits to my thighs to draw attention to my royal-purple, cowl-neck sheath dress. Sure, it's on the tighter side and it shows off the bottom half of my legs nicely (especially paired with my favorite Jimmys), but it goes all the way to my knees and there's no cleavage to be seen.

My hunch is that fifty-something-year-old Miranda —who would be very beautiful herself if she'd let up on the snarl—is jealous.

I mean, I *do* have a great body. (What? It's good to be confident in what you've got.) But I'd never put another woman down or judge her for what she wore. (Evie was different, by the way! I wasn't judging her clothing choices per se. More the fact that she was hiding herself and needed to be given permission to show off a bit.)

Josh is still floundering like a fish, his mouth gaping open. I've clearly embarrassed him with my question. "You know what? Never mind." I pick up my card and sink onto a stool lining one side of the counter.

He recovers quickly, grabbing a cup and writing my name across the yellow surface. Looks like he's taking orders and making the drinks today all by his lonesome.

"Where's Hannah?" The other barista, a pretty blonde, is usually here too when I come in.

"Family in town." Turning, he squirts a good squeeze of chocolate syrup all around the cup. Cocks his head. "More?"

I nod. Eating (or drinking, rather) my feelings isn't great, I know, but desperate times. I'll attend one of Lauren's crazy cycling classes tomorrow morning to make up for it.

He adds another good dose then gets the grinder going. Its whirring fills the air, and there's something mildly calming about it. I watch Josh's hands move in a pattern I've seen a thousand times: measure, click, push, pull, pour, froth, mix, squirt.

My heart rate steadies.

And when he slides the cup in front of me, I immediately take a sip and groan as the sweet, bold flavor rides my tongue all the way down my throat. Then I say the first thing that pops into my brain. "I could kiss you right now."

He coughs and takes off his glasses, running the edge of his T-shirt over the lenses. "Well, I hope it helps your rough day get a little smoother." He's so darn bashful, and I feel bad for rattling him with my unfiltered talk.

"It will." Standing, I pull a few dollars from my wallet and stuff them into the tip jar next to the register. "Have a good weekend, Josh. I'll see you Monday."

"See you." A pause. "And Kayla? It's not inappropriate. The sexy dress. I mean …" He rubs the back of his neck and turns the color of a crisp fall apple.

Laughing, I shake my head and raise my cup to him. "You're the best, Josh."

I'm still chuckling at the adorable barista as I drive to my destination. I'd already arranged to be off this afternoon, so my trip to Java Awakening after my run-in with Miranda was well-timed.

Turning off the ignition, I finish off my mocha and climb from the vehicle in front of the cute little house. The For Sale sign is gone and there are two cars in the driveway. My heels click against the sidewalk as I throw open the eggshell-blue front door. "Honey, I'm home!"

"Back here!" Evie shouts.

The house is minuscule—less than a thousand square feet—and it's got a lot of things that need fixing, but as of today, it belongs to my best friend and I couldn't be happier for her. She put in the offer the day after her boss gave her back her promotion (and the day she and Connor reunited), and here she is, six weeks later, a homeowner.

I'm glad at least one of us has her life together, especially because she's loving her new position as associate publisher. She misses working with Connor, but apparently he has enough money in savings to take a year off and try to make it as a full-time author.

It takes me zero point two seconds to walk through the great room and kitchen area, down the hall, and into the bedroom, where Evie and Connor are sitting on a blanket in the middle of the otherwise empty floor.

And surprise, surprise—they're kissing, even though they know I'm in the house.

I kick at a dust bunny the size of my big toe and lean against the bedroom door frame. "Should I come back another time?"

Evie breaks away, laughing. "Sorry."

"What she means is sorry, *not* sorry." Connor loops his arm around her waist and tugs her to his side.

Rolling my eyes but smiling, I spot a bottle of champagne and three flutes behind them. "A bit of bubbly to celebrate the move in?" Although actually, Evie won't be moving in until she gets things fixed up around here. But it won't be long till she's out and Alexis finds another roomie to replace her.

Not that anyone could ever replace her. Something twists in my gut at the thought.

"That and"—Evie looks at Connor with shining pride in her eyes—"Connor got a two-book deal!"

"Seriously?" I plop onto the blanket beside them, extending my legs in front of me and crossing them at the ankles. "Didn't you just sign with an agent? I thought the process was usually long and drawn out."

"Yeah." He pops the champagne and starts pouring. The fizz takes up half the flute, then recedes. "I got lucky."

"Luck may have been part of it, but it took a ton of hard work and focus and talent. There was even an auction, which means a ton of houses were fighting over it." Evie grins as she takes one of the flutes and hands it to me.

The chill of the glass bleeds through my fingers. I love these two together. I love seeing my friend so happy.

But I'll never be as happy as her, because I'll never be as good as she is. And that's not me being all "woe is me, I'm not worthy." I just recognize (and accept) that she's a better person than me who sees the good in others.

That will never be me. I've seen too much pain in my own life, and the life of others, to ever really fall in love. (I spend a ton of my time working divorce cases and there's nothing like that to make you see the seedier side of humanity—and supposed love.)

Other than Evie, I'm not convinced there are many truly good people in the world.

Definitely not guys.

Especially guys who would like *me*. I'm too forthright, too intimidating, too … much.

That's all right, though. When Evie and Connor

inevitably get married and have gorgeous babies, I'll be the best darn auntie anyone has ever seen. I'll teach their daughters how to wear makeup and be confident in what they bring to the table, and I'll teach their sons how to talk to girls the right way.

Tucking my hair behind my ear, I lift my glass in the air. "To Connor and Evie, the world's most adorable couple. To Connor, the soon-to-be-published author. And to Evs—may this little house bring you years of joy and laughter, because you deserve it." I choke on the words. *Do not cry, Kayla Clark. You are not a crier.* "You deserve it all."

And as my best friend *ahhhs* and leans in to kiss her man, I toss back my champagne and embrace the bubbles' biting sting against my tongue.

Thanks so much for reading *Loving the Ladies' Man*. If you enjoyed Connor and Evie's story, please consider leaving a review.

Want to find out what happens with Kayla and Josh? Check out their story in *Desiring His Dating Coach*.

Want a little more of Evie and Connor's happily ever after? Download the *Loving the Ladies' Man* Bonus Epilogue at kristincanary.com/LTLM.

sneak peek

Desiring His Dating Coach

If adults had staring contests, I would be the queen.

But right now, inside the conference room at Jamison and Associates, I finally have a worthy opponent—although "worthy" is a term I use loosely.

Miranda Jamison (aka my boss, aka the Wicked Witch) stands at the front of the room, her lithe fifty-something-year-old body tucked and nipped to perfection, her narrowed violet eyes zeroed in on me. "You cannot be serious, Kayla."

The modern-chic space—with its plush carpet, large oak table, and floor-to-ceiling window that gives a gorgeous view of San Diego Bay—suddenly feels a lot warmer. A lot smaller.

But it doesn't matter that someone definitely turned up the thermostat in here or that the table is surrounded by twelve other attorneys (all men).

To break eye contact is to concede defeat.

So, rather than shrinking like some sort of wilted

flower, I cross my arms over my green silk blouse and black blazer, doing my best to look intimidating despite my rather petite 5'5" frame. "I stand by what I said. If you don't settle that case ASAP, Mrs. Lincoln has no hope of getting custody of her children."

Miranda's not-a-gray-hair-in-sight brown bob shifts as she cocks her head and studies me like a spider must observe its next meal. But news flash, sister. I'm nobody's lunch. She may have pushed me around for the last seven years when I was desperate for a job so I could repay my massive law school student loans, but those puppies have been paid off for two months now. I am so done with holding back while Miranda berates me and gives all the promotions to my male colleagues —even when they don't deserve it.

Oh yeah, did you hear the part where Miranda and I are the only female attorneys at the upper-crust divorce and family law firm she owns? You'd think that would bond us together. Instead, it seems to have put me in her constant crosshairs. And lately, it's only gotten worse.

A smile curves across Miranda's unrealistically smooth face. At her age, there's no way she shouldn't have a few wrinkles. I wish she'd let them show instead of BOTOX-ing the crap out of her forehead, nose, mouth, and who knows where else. It would make her appear more human. (Although we all know that appearances can be deceiving …)

"What does everyone else think? Do you agree with Ms. Clark? Should we just abandon our client in her time of need, when she's come to us for assistance?"

Daniel, another attorney who has been vying for an

open junior partner position alongside *moi*, leans forward in the seat next to me. The air is thick with his expensive cologne, and I can't help but admire the cut of his Armani suit. Like all Jamison and Associates attorneys, he knows the importance of looking one's best at all times (even if there's an unfortunate and hefty price tag attached to the requirement). And with his rocking bod and styled blond hair, he does. Those muscles bulging beneath the suit coat aren't hurting anything either.

Then he opens his mouth and all the charm vanishes. "I think your plan to double down and push back is a brilliant one," Daniel says, grinning at Miranda like she invented Cross Fit, which he pretty much talks about nonstop because it's his "favorite hobby." (Sorry, but exercise is not a hobby—it's a necessity, and only a psycho would say otherwise.)

All around me, the men mumble their agreement. Looks like I'm standing alone. Again.

A snarky reply is on the tip of my tongue, but I bite it back. Yes, I may refer to Miranda as the Wicked Witch around my friends when I'm frustrated, but I also recognize that she *is* the boss. So even though she's done absolutely nothing to deserve it, by default I will do my utmost to show her respect.

Which means, for now, I drop eye contact and clench my teeth as Miranda covers a few other items from the agenda. My phone buzzes on the table and I peek down at a text from my mother.

Your father called. Again. He really wants me to give you his number, so here it is. I'm only giving it to you so he will stop calling me, because apparently blocking his number does no good. Do with it what you will.

For the last three months, the dad who left when I was a kid has been trying to weasel his way back into my life via my mother. I swipe the notification away and focus on the meeting because I refuse to give the man another thought, another minute of my time. I've wasted too many years on him already.

Miranda finally dismisses the group to our afternoon midweek work. Thank goodness, because my standing coffee date at Java Awakening with my best friend and roomie Evie is calling my name. I snag my purse from my office then head toward the front lobby.

Jennifer, the receptionist who has been working here for a little over a month, waves hello from her desk. "How was the meeting today?"

I arch an eyebrow. "Swell."

Jennifer laughs. "That good, huh?" Taking a quick peek around the empty lobby, she leans closer. "How goes Project Get-Me-a-Date?"

"That name needs some serious work, you know." But I laugh in spite of myself, allowing the tension from the meeting to roll off of my shoulders and away. "I'm still looking for the perfect guy for you. Don't worry. I'm a pro."

My housemates tease me about my ability to know which celebrity couples (and real-life ones) will make it and which won't, and I've helped set more than one friend up on dates.

Jennifer nibbles her bottom lip. "Just remember, I don't look like you."

"So?" She's right—my shoulder-length highlighted brown locks are nothing like her bright red curls, and her tall frame has a lot more curves than mine—but she says it like it's a bad thing. I don't get it, though, because she's beautiful and sweet and any man would be lucky to have her. I just haven't found him yet.

But I will not give up, because that's not something I do.

Jennifer looks down at her desk. "*So …* the guys who would say yes to *you* wouldn't even glance at me twice."

"Believe me, you don't want the kind of guy who would say yes to me."

"You mean rich, sexy, and an amazing kisser?" She looks at me and sighs. "No, I don't want a man like *that* at all."

I laugh. "How about conceited and only interested in one thing? No, you deserve a guy who actually wants a relationship, who cares about you on a deeper level, who sees you as more than someone to have fun with." Although honestly, I like fun. Fun keeps things low pressure—and it keeps my heart safe. "And those guys can be sexy and good kissers too."

Not that I'd know from experience, which has shown that most guys who are actually worth having a relationship with are intimidated by my strong personality. Even though they might say they want a woman who doesn't play games, apparently they don't like it when a woman is tooooo blunt or has no filter or calls them on their crap. (Go figure.)

"Well, I'm sure if anyone can find such a mythical unicorn for me in San Diego, you can." Jennifer grins as three of the male attorneys breeze past us, laughing and joking like good old boys. Daniel is one of them, and as he opens the glass front door, he turns and winks at me before leaving for what I assume is a late lunch.

"Looks like someone has a crush on our Kayla," Jennifer says as she fiddles with some pens in a container on her desk.

"Gag me."

"What? He's dreamy. With the way his eyes are always on you, I'm shocked he hasn't asked you out yet."

"Oh, he has. Three times." One of them just this morning, in fact.

"And you said no? Why? Not your type?"

"He's handsome, sure, but I can't stomach his arrogance." And there's an even bigger reason I won't go out with him. "I also don't date co-workers."

Unlike Evie, who recently fell in love with a guy she worked with for ten years, I find the whole idea much too messy. There are too many potential variables to take into consideration, too many things that could go wrong.

Too many things outside of my control.

"Hmm. Okay." Jennifer considers me. "By the way, in addition to finding me a date, do you think maybe you could give me a makeover and help me like you helped your other friend?"

A few months ago, Evie became my special project. We worked on building her confidence in order to land a promotion—and in the process, she also landed her boyfriend, Connor. "Of course I'll help you. Let's figure out a time to get together soon."

"Thanks, Kayla. You're awesome." She points at the clock on her desk. "You'd better go if you want to make your coffee date. Say hello to that yummy barista for me while you're there."

I lift my eyebrows. "Who, Josh?"

"Mmm hmm."

Yummy, huh? Jennifer went with me last week to pick up drinks for a client meeting, but she never mentioned that she thought Josh was cute. Although with his boy-next-door good looks, I'm not surprised. "Maybe he would be a nice match for you."

"I don't know. It looked like he might be into you."

I wave the suggestion away. "That's just silly." The guy is quiet and sweet, and I'm kind of the opposite of that. I doubt he'd be attracted to my particular brand of crazy. "You two, though … I'll have to see if he's single."

"But—"

"See ya!" I turn on my heel to head out the door, but hear a hideous sound behind me—the clearing of a throat.

Her throat.

"Kayla."

In slow motion, I round to find Miranda standing in the lobby's opening. "Yes?" I say as sweetly as I possibly can. (I should be given some sort of acting award, people. My words are dripping with freaking molasses.)

"I need to speak with you." She crooks a finger at me like I'm a naughty student being summoned to the principal's office. "Now."

"Can it wait? I'm supposed to meet ..." But my words die off at the pinched look on her face. I sigh and pull my phone from my purse, dashing out a text to Evie: *Wicked Witch wants to meet. Gonna be late. Will text when I'm on the way.*

Then I follow Miranda, my four-inch Jimmy Choos sounding my doom down the wood-floored hallway.

When we get inside her office, she closes the door and indicates that I should take a seat. "I assume you know what this is about."

"No, actually I don't."

She sits across from me behind her desk and steeples her long thin fingers together under her chin. Her features could be beautiful if she used her powers for good and not evil. Instead, she resembles a hawk with eyes narrowed and plump lips pursed (like a beak curled and ready to peck me to death). "It's true. There are *so many* things we need to discuss. Your insolence during today's meeting, for example."

My cheeks are blazing as bees start buzzing in my ears. She has no idea how much I held back during that meeting. Or maybe she does, and she's just testing me now.

But I will not explode. She's pushed me further than this and hasn't broken me yet. "I'm sorry you felt I was being insolent. You asked for my opinion, and I gave it." I keep my voice nice and controlled. Steady.

Take that, Wicked Witch. (What? I never said I was mature in my own head.)

She sighs. "Then there's the matter of your clothing.

I thought we'd discussed last week how you were going to wear outfits that were more … professional."

What happened to women uplifting one another? Yes, we had a "discussion" last Friday, when she berated my clothing choices in front of the entire staff. I glance down at my blouse and skirt. The shirt is not low-cut in the slightest and the pencil skirt, while hugging my curves, goes all the way to my knees when I'm standing up.

It's not as if her clothes are much different. I just don't understand the double standard. Perhaps she can enlighten me. "About that—"

"But what I actually called you in here to discuss today is this. I have it on good authority that you continue to ask Daniel out, almost to the point of harassment," Miranda says. "And we just can't abide that kind of behavior here, Kayla."

I'm sorry, what? I shoot out of my chair. "I haven't asked him out. *He's* asked *me* out multiple times, despite multiple no's on my part."

"Even if that was true, I'm sure you encouraged him in some way or he wouldn't keep asking."

The utter gall of this woman. "And just how do you suppose I did that?"

"I believe I mentioned your clothing choices."

Oh, we're going there, are we? My hands become fists at my side. "So you think that if a man can't help but harass me, it's my own fault because of what I'm wearing—which isn't even unprofessional, I might add? What is this, 1950?"

"Please don't shout, Kayla." She's trying to hold back a grin. I can tell by the brightness in her eyes, the same one she gets when she's closing in on an opponent in the courtroom—like a shark on the hunt for wounded prey. *Well, I'm not bleeding, lady, so back off.* "I still find it difficult to believe that Daniel would make all of this up."

"Of course he's making it up. He's trying to take the junior partnership away from me!"

She laughs, a trill that burns a fire in my belly. "For that to happen, it would have to be yours in the first place. And, I'm sorry to say it, but at this time you are not one of my top choices for the position."

I sink back into my chair. "What?" Seriously? After all the hours I've put in, all the ways I've dedicated myself to this job, all the ways I've gone above and beyond, she doesn't even see me as a contender? What about the time I was working mere hours after I got my appendix out—all while still in the hospital? Or the time I canceled my vacation at Christmas to cover a last-minute case that no one else wanted?

Or the many, many all-nighters I've pulled when the co-workers *she* promoted didn't do their jobs?

I guess I shouldn't be surprised, though. Miranda has never liked me. And yet ... "Why?"

The back of my eyelids burn, but there's no way I'm giving her the satisfaction of crying over this. *"Never let them see you cry, Kayla. It's weakness, pure and simple."* My mom's words from childhood wend their way inside me, bolstering me, feeding my determination.

"Are the things I've just covered with you not enough reason?" She sighs, shaking her head like she pities me. "You are a brilliant woman, Kayla. I only wish you'd spend a little less time looking down on everyone else and a little more time doing your job."

I sit there, feeling like a concrete roller has just flattened me. How could she say that? She *knows* what it's like to be a woman in today's workforce, especially in the world of law—how we're expected to not only have it all together but appear equal parts fierce enough to win for our clients and yet somehow soft enough to nurture and build relationships.

But it only takes a moment for the spark of her words to ignite into a raging fire that consumes all of me. And I realize in this moment that I'd rather be fed to a sarlacc by Jabba the Hut than keep working for Miranda. I don't need this job anymore—not like I used to.

And I don't need her.

"I quit."

Miranda rears back—but how can she really be surprised? "Excuse me?"

"You heard me." I stand without even a wobble. Because yes, this is right. And I should have done it a long time ago. "This is a toxic environment. You're a sexist. And I'm done here."

books by kristin canary

California Dreamin' Series

Enamoring Her Amnesic Ex (prequel)

Loving the Ladies' Man

Desiring His Dating Coach

Saving the Secret Prince

Belonging With Her Best Friend

Engaging the Office Enemy

Needing the Next-Door Neighbor

Hallmark Beach Series

Beachside Kisses With My Bodyguard

about the author

Kristin is a wife and boy mom who functions best on peach tea and cookie dough ice cream. A desert dweller, she always has her eye on the next trip to a beach somewhere—and if she can't travel there in person, then you'd better believe she's going to write about it. Kristin is never fully satisfied with a movie, TV show, or book without a hefty dose of romance in it, and she's grateful to be living a true-life love story with her own crazy little family. Connect with her at KristinCanary.com.

facebook.com/kristincanary
instagram.com/kristincanaryauthor